W9-BDL-640

The Incantation of Frida K.

The Incantation of Frida K.

KATE BRAVERMAN

SEVEN STORIES PRESS

New York   Toronto   London   Sydney

A Seven Stories Press First Edition

Seven Stories Press
140 Watts Street
New York NY 10013
www.sevenstories.com

In Canada: Hushion House, 36 Northline Road, Toronto Ontario M4B 3E2

In the U.K.: Turnaround Publishing Services Ltd., Unit 3, Olympia Trading Estate, Coburg Road, Wood Green, London N22 6TZ

In Australia: Tower Books, 9/19 Rodborough Road, Frenchs Forest NSW 2086

Library of Congress Cataloging-in-Publication Data
Braverman, Kate.
        The Incantation of Frida K / Kate Braverman.—A Seven Stories Press 1st ed.
        p. cm.
        ISBN 1-58322-469-6
        1. Kahlo, Frida—Fiction. 2. Rivera, Diego, 1886–1957—Fiction. 3.
Painters' spouses—Fiction. 4. Women painters—Fiction. 5. Mexico—Fiction.
I. Title.
PS3552.R3555 C66 2001
813'.54—dc21
                                                            2001006795

9 8 7 6 5 4 3 2 1

College professors may order examination copies of Seven Stories Press titles for a free six-month trial period. To order, visit www.sevenstories.com/textbook, or fax on school letterhead to (212) 226-1411.

Book design by M. Astella Saw

Printed in the U.S.A.

ACKNOWLEDGEMENTS

I acknowledge the following for their inspiration and the indelible intersections of our destinies. I am grateful for my family, my husband, Alan, and my daughter, Gabrielle. In addition, Danielle Roter, Gerald Rosen, Jack Kleinberg, Bob Quinn, Thomas Preston, Mary Donovan, Dave Diamond, Michael Clark, Sallie O'Neill, my students, Momentum Press, Illuminati Press, the UCLA Writer's Program, Beyond Baroque, and the Venice Poetry Workshop. For this book, I am particularly indebted to the Alfred community, Amy Scholder, and Jill Schoolman.

FOR MY BROTHER, HANK

In this net it's not just the strings that count
But also the air that escapes through the meshes.

PABLO NERUDA

I WAS BORN IN RAIN and I will die in rain. Know me as river, as harbor. They will say I was a slut with a brazen sailor's mouth. They will not remember my elegance and restraint. They will say they looked in my eyes and counted one hundred forty-six pelicans flying in a wavering line into a marina at sunset.

Men don't have the vocabulary for such eyes. A brown, calculating and predatory. Men lack the spectrum, the palette. It is not the eyes themselves, but rather what they contain, the vision. Diego is like that, with his compulsion to categorize. Men prefer primitive bodies outlined with hard black edges like the Maya painted.

I resist the obvious borders. For this heresy I have been categorically penalized. Did you know they sealed me into a cast for one entire year? It was a premature burial where I kept breathing under dirt. They did this repeatedly, gathered my crushed bones like wildflowers and used plaster as a vase. They sought to make an object of me. There was no composition. It was vandalism.

I learned, in a hospital, in one solitary confinement or another, that it is still an era of barbarism. In surgery and convalescent rooms, laminated by electric light, I recognized their limitations. They are bloated with ambition, but their methods are inadequate. This knowledge is an illumination that burns. It is the essence of genius and affliction.

In this way I transcended them. I defied gravity. I should have died in the gutter like a barren dog, a hit-by-trolley-car bitch. I should have died in Diego's overwhelming shadow, curled into its shallows and currents. Its bloodstained coral reefs. Who but a water woman could have navigated his mined ports? He was a lady-killer. He murdered me slowly. It took him decades of sabotage. But wind and infection outwitted him.

This is the reason for the grief he will flagrantly display. He will mourn, but it will be with a theatrical and unsettling ambiguity. He will recall my parrot cage torso and nights of sleeping on razors and barbed wire. He will find the place where they sawed off my leg. He will dream it, how it smelled like decayed meat in a dirt alley at noon in a region of drought and plague, dust, piss of goats, rot of hibiscus. Diego will recognize the trolley car has stopped. He may mistake my absence for freedom.

They will say I smoked cigarettes and marijuana, cursed hoarse as a crow in all my languages and loved morphine and Demerol, tequila and pulque, women and men. I will shrug my illusion of shoulders and answer that I am a water woman, not a vessel, not something you can sail or charter. I am instead the tributary, the river, the fluid source, and the sea itself. I am all her rainy implications. And what do you, with your rusted compass, know of love?

Their grafts and amputations, the casts and operations, are without limit. They will not complete their excavations, for surely I am an archaeological site now, not a woman, not a human, not anymore. When you have survived the withering disease, when you have dragged your polio leg like an anomalous branch scratching the pavement behind you, when you have continued breathing after they left you for dead on a city boulevard, when you have lived with Diego, when you have looked into your face and seen your third eye, you know death is a reward.

When they have skinned me completely, I will be as water women freed of their unnecessary bodies. Men prescribe these structures, these female forms, for pleasure and convenience and the perpetuation of sons. They invent laws and rituals to enforce this. I have taught myself to become deaf to them, oblivious. Of course, it's been a mutual decision. Mine has not been a typical exile but rather a negotiated settlement. I left the world as it is ordinarily known and it left me.

When they cease the medieval procedures they call medicine, progress, and technology, I will float like a leaf, a delinquent maple beginning to curl, to turn to tissue to be painted on. I could etch the surface. I have the tools. I am as intelligent as they are and more subtle.

Yes. I am screaming. It's time for morphine. I hear cathedral bells through rain. It's the hour for amnesia and invisibility I call being saved. Nurse better come.

I will be like a sheet of parchment on which is printed a chemical formula for immortality. Or perhaps it is a prayer by an adept, a bruja's incantation for the end of pain. Or an American doctor's prescription. Or a prophecy announcing the obliteration of obsolete forms, like promises and political systems of social justice, and the more exquisite personal savagery called marriage.

I understand what floats on rivers which conclude in harbors pale as the veins of infants. What you see from your veranda is not debris but entire texts rendered intelligible. This is what moves in the current, on the backs of stray fronds, the sodden bleached lily and old newspapers. Cures for insomnia and betrayal by man and accident. And methods to heal abscesses and find lost daughters.

I consider a journey through the fluid called a continuum. A physicist at a dinner party in London explained this to me. He said you could cross it, this construct, like a continent or an ocean. We have just not yet devised vehicles for the passage. We are too primitive.

I experienced joy then. It was England and I drank too much tequila and brandy. I wanted to remove my Tehauna dress with its stiff ruffles and embroidered stylized flowers. I longed to dance barefoot, skirt dropped to the floor. I still had two feet then. But my withered leg made me shy as a child.

I wanted to tell the scientist it was still the Dark Ages. Perhaps I was too drunk. The ninth century, the nineteenth. A trivial difference. How many will there be? Incoherent centuries, ruled by irrational hunger? A thousand, perhaps? Ten thousand?

How can I know this, as rain falls and bells fall and dissolve, and petals and moths and stars? I am pagan. You cannot get to my birthplace simply by booking passage and having your passport in order. There are doors where your stamps and visas are rejected absolutely. Some points of entry are deceptive. The currency and conditions for admission are in constant fluctuation, like a woman dreaming. Perhaps you must offer human flesh, or gardenias out of season. Or butterflies in jars collected by crippled children in alleys dense with the scent of jasmine and urine and a sense that a woman has been recently slapped.

You can see this clearly in what I paint. This is not a journal imposed on canvas, not a chronicle of disasters. That would be banal. Instead, I revealed alternative ports of entry and exit. I crossed bridges where there were none. I possessed a fluid intuition like a stillborn ocean. I was singled out. I was taken to the place where no official papers are required.

They will say, what did you paint, Frida? What did you mean? What were your intentions? There are words you don't need a mouth for. I was investigating my numerous faces and chance identities. My transitory improvisational versions of myself. They were mere approximations, so peripheral and distant, so poor the translation, they had nothing to do with me. That is how you discover truth. In half-light, by accident, when you meant to simply reach down and retrieve a leaf. You notice it looks etched, engraved, ornamental as a religious script. Your fingers stutter. You drop the leaf to the ground and think, suddenly, of arthritis.

Did I say stones know too much? Did I say church bells are ringing? Someone is supposed to bring me a vial, a crystal filled with amethyst. Is Nurse coming?

They will say, she wore flowers, hair a bouquet of intricate ribbons. She dressed as if for a fiesta. Listen. That is not the case. I wore gardens pinned to my head like floral tumors rising from my brain. I wore orchids not in celebration, but in mourning. I prepared daily for my funeral. I painted myself with birds and monkeys, with a necklace of thorns, and with the well where my heart should be gouged out, as if by scalpel.

I was not painting my interior diary. I was not painting myself thinking. It had nothing to do with symbols. I lived as if posthumously. It's a gift, to slide through edges, to know the properties of light within pewter and silver like ordinary women know the geography of a country.

I was in perpetual pause. A stasis where I memorized lies. Insomnia is identical in all seasons, rancid as soiled bandages, the pus on gauze. I am opening my mouth to eat this night and the cathedral bells, which are dissolving like worthless artifacts. But Nurse is coming. She is bringing me amethysts and a sundial I can swallow.

Did I tell you, Diego tried to kill me? Marriage was simply a context. It let me make my wounds specific. Diego made the world simple. He was cause and effect.

Diego had the heart of a butcher. He had the hands of an executioner before metal or bullets, when men killed with their fingers, for pleasure. But Diego moved slowly. His strategies were transparent. He was like his paintings, enormous but too obvious.

"This is what I do. This is the work of a man," Diego would laugh from his scaffold when he was creating murals in Mexico City, or San Francisco, Detroit, or New York. "Your paintings are diminutive. You are like women who paint flowers on plates. Women who embroider pillows. You are decorative."

"They are small but potent. They are a visual curare," I would answer. I still bothered to speak his dialect, to make my lips conform to the borders men insist are really there. "You are monumental but simple," I would say. "I am layered and cryptic. More deceptive than you suspect."

Diego laughed at me. He painted the status quo. He took their consensual point of view. He lacked spontaneity and daring. He did not invent his own perspective. Eventually, he would be unmasked and discarded. It was the force of his personality alone that made him famous. Poor Diego, convinced applause was a warm breath of echo, an embrace you can keep. When his face was gone, his voice and millionaire connections buried, when the edifice of his personal celebrity was erased, his canvases would be without surprise.

After the war, after Hiroshima and the concentration camps, the palette expanded in dimension. Diego did not notice. Then I knew murals would be as debris, ash, a flare of gray and then nothing.

"You idiot," Diego shouted, defending himself. "One must be a newspaper event to even become a footnote to history now."

I considered Diego's murals. It was an American autumn. The trees were like cathedrals in late afternoon sun, one cold snap and a rain from collapse. When Diego spoke of history, as if he owned it, I felt a serrated knife was gouging out my eye.

Perhaps it was Detroit. Diego stopped working, overwhelmed by his achievement, his engineering and architectural prowess, his buckets, ropes, measuring instruments, chemicals, blueprints, and paints. "Treated properly, they will last fifty thousand years."

Detroit. I could still see where I was, though it took an astounding act of flamboyant amber to do it. A colossal maple. It refused to compromise. It waited for me to come from Mexico. A maple, a staggering burgundy. I could get drunk from the bark. Oaks at the horizon. A stand with browning leaves, almost a dull plum, in a ridge like a spine or an anchor. Maybe I won't drown.

"Frida," my new husband said. He pointed his arm. "Conceive of fifty thousand years."

How long will your murals last now, with the atom bomb? Is there even a construction of events now, as we once knew it? No, Diego. No more certainties. Only temporary pandering on a ragged machine-gunned stage, a few tunes and anonymous breasts in a grim dusk. Then they blow the candles out and with them, your canvases and newspaper clippings, even the cement walls and steel girders of your buildings.

Silence. Autumn let herself in. The air was crinoline, campanile bells, a hard rain like a glassy hail and women in song, opening their throats to Jesus. I refused to speak. There was the fragrance of street lamps and the stall of wind.

Perhaps it was later. We were partners in a family business. We could have been selling tomatoes and sacks of mangoes in a tienda at a narrowing in an alley below a plaza. We could have been squatting on muddy burlap, weighing out handfuls of cilantro.

Now our languages diverged. Diego and I were tribes living on different sides of a river. Our vocabulary had been minimal from the beginning, almost conceptual, really. Soon we would not speak at all, grunt and howl and hit each other with sticks.

I was a guerrilla. I struck from beneath my huipil and rebozo, my turquoise and silver squash blossoms, my amulets of Aztec deities. Coatlicue, Tezcatlipoca, and Tlaloc, mother of the brood. I was a sort of ambulatory tree. I was the home of parrots and monkeys. I was a festering nest. I painted myself with vines growing from my hollowed chest and seashells for organs. I put sharp points and hummingbirds around my neck. I drove more than sixty-seven nails into my hips and chest.

I deciphered a dialect for renegade women, exiled and escaped women. My paintings are postcards sent from ports not yet identified. I know where they are. San Francisco is one, Detroit, and New York. I put cactus in my heavens, agave and century plants. Heaven is a desert. The vegetation is sparse, brutal with concealed spikes. An occasional human passes parched and bereft. They open their palms, discover stigmata. Now they know what to eat. They stand like saguaro and joshua trees, amnesiac in the blaze, paralyzed, reciting litanies that feel like gravel in their throats.

I was born in the Casa Azul in Coyoacán, the color of a child's first chalked sky, and I will die there. It will be raining a partial blue of lilacs and suggestion. A shy rain. A crippled virgin's rain. The rain drifts, a mesh the scent of a singer's bones. Women who master certain sounds can change their body parts, their morphologies. All syllables begin as visual signals. This is verbal alchemy and why they are called blues singers.

It is raining this afternoon, chipped aqua defining the eggshell edges of my existence. One storm straying into another like so many confused dogs. They are barking now, our Itzcuintli, past the veranda, in soaked foliage.

Dog. They said I smelled like a sick dog. When they sawed off the body cast that they called, with curious irony, a corset, they found the wounds that didn't heal, the abscesses. They said I emitted an odor like a scorched horse. I was what remained in the village two weeks after the troops move on, in an exceptionally hot August, when there is nothing left to rape. Even the girl children look dangerous, dazed, thick white foam like meringue hangs from their mouths. They have pinpoint eyes, stained skirts, no shoes. They limp in dirt, cough, look contagious. Bodies spread out like offerings in the bombed plazas, starving dogs eat their thighs, wolves creep in from the forests which have been burned.

This was the tableau on my back. A nurse vomited in the corridor. That was the hospital in Mexico City where my toes, my charcoal toes that I had been hiding like my ten bastard babies, fell off on their own accord. I had kept them attached by sheer will. Then they cut off my shoes, scalpel though leather. The gasp and emergency conference. Then they said I had gangrene.

Nurses ran from me. This is the odor of garbage and war, someone said. I considered a city after a long summer siege. Papayas, burros piss down a gully where used gauze has been tossed and children are sitting, drawing numbers with their fingers in mud

"Do I smell like an animal?" I ask Diego. He's wearing a new Panama hat. He has brought me both flowers and chocolates.

Diego bends over me. He removes his white hat, closes his eyes, breathes me in. "You are like citrus," he says. "Sweet lemon. Oranges."

"You are a disappointment as a liar," I say. But I know he cannot penetrate this moment. I paint nerves in the process of evolving, connecting into complexities of jungle, into one radiant purity. Diego paints buildings.

I look into his bloated face, the face that seems sabotaged, artificially enlarged. I realize he is a creature of the surface, like certain defective insects. It is his defining characteristic. If he could devise a further language, he would be a master, rather than a fashionable mediocrity.

"You bring your accidents with you. It's your gift," Diego said, voice soft. "You smell like a zoo or the circus."

A circus. A girl on an elephant in gold sequins, rough costume jewelry, but not without a certain singularity. Last night, she dreamt of huge plums, a picnic perhaps, with extravagant baskets of berries. Her lover throws a knife smuggled from Turkey, the handle a soft European gold filigree. And the sisters on the trapeze, in some sweaty celestial trajectory.

Diego brought his predictable geometry with him. When he looked at a field, he saw corn stalks or grapes or calla lilies. He saw women embracing sunflowers. He did not see walking skeletons or infants hideous with tendrils growing through their orifices. Or women wearing velvet gowns lounging on crevices that look like machete blades in flesh. My deserts had avenues carved in by acid. Diego did not know that landscape is a character with its own motives and destiny. He looked at a field and saw plants, not a forest where deer with women's faces ran struck by arrows.

His frescos depicted men working, men and their machines, their recognizable activities and postures. Diego had the consistency that invites commissions. He was a salesman. He could even ensure media coverage, like a soccer championship or an election. Diego did not know time is a river. It did not occur to him.

"You smell like California," Diego finally said. We were smoking in the hospital in Mexico City.

"Fuck you. You're a small man. You have no imagination," I told him. I had pulque and tequila. I had morphine hidden in the bedding, in my clothing, but I didn't need it. They injected me with Demerol every two hours. I did not have to beg or scream or navigate by bells like I do now at Casa Azul.

"Your companionship reduces me," I told Diego.

"Everyone comes to that. It's inevitable," Diego admitted. He seemed sad.

My hand resembled the fin of a marine mammal. It wasn't gnarled. It was simply losing its definition, blurring into the water that ran through rooms and made the air too moist. There were spruces in the doorway. Acres of shadowy moss on the floors. In the corridors, oaks and birches. I must be at a high altitude, I realized. That would explain the lingering scent of wet leaves. And why my nose was bleeding.

Soft slide of the syringe. Demerol autumn. The light is clarified and redeemed. The cobalt sky is naked, like remote inland seas that still bear their original names. This is what the last breath of a heart seizure must be, pastel and iris. You understand the condensed narratives inside stone. And you don't need a wedding ring.

I thought of our first Christmas in America, in San Francisco. That's when I learned the tradition of kissing under mistletoe. Diego needed no excuse. He kissed everybody. His mouth was a confusion of sherry and vanilla, lemon and strong tea. His mouth was filled with what you do not see in the mirror, what you do not tell the priest. What you do not tell your wife.

Diego presented me with a diamond bracelet. An accessory for a concubine. Its glare rendered me silent. That was his intention.

I would study it in the long winter nights when he was gone, when he was with other women, aristocrats with blond hair, strawberry blond, platinum blond, ash blond, dirty blond. It was his winter of blond women, tailored, with fur collars on their coats, mink at their throat, small animals trying to claw their way free. Their dead feet dangled. These women were patrons of the arts. Women with red sports cars and special outfits for riding horses and going on safaris in Africa. Women who could shoot guns and ski.

"We must adapt," Diego would say. "We must be international."

Diego was changing his shirt, in one hotel suite or another. The wallpaper was a perpetual fist-size pink floral print, miles of it, from one city to another, as if we hadn't actually traveled anywhere. The enamel lamp was turned on. It looked like teeth stained by nicotine.

I examined his diamond offering by lamplight and sunlight. There is an anatomy in diamonds, in their elegant flares. Such stones could burn my wrists and linger infected. I would have dog arms. Isn't that why we wear amulets? For the implication of metamorphosis, of sudden new identities? One could remember differently. That's why they were so costly, why people thought them valuable.

It was the season of Diego's blond americanas. I was alone in San Francisco. My bracelet became my friend. The diamonds were mirrored chambers. From certain angles, augury was possible. I drank tequila and brandy. Tequila made rooms turn amber, like honey and lanterns. I could read the future. I stared at my wrist and made predictions about love and drowning, babies and lightning.

In San Francisco, my cold became pneumonia, two ribs broke, a bone in my back shook loose from my relentless coughing. Confined to bed, I created stories in the mirrors I wore. I looked at my wrist and saw trains in charcoal stations where the language was harsh and I didn't understand the coins or how to negotiate passage from the depot to the port.

Years later, I walked along a harbor smelling of cinnamon and cloves and kelp. At a pier at the end of wood pilings past fishermen and painters with easels and negligible ambition, I dropped the bracelet into the sea. It was contaminated. It had nothing to do with love. When Diego asked me to wear it, I claimed it was lost, an accident, a casualty of travel.

"I threw your bracelet away," I say to Diego now. He has come with Nurse. A silver tray covered with a white cloth. One lily in a bud vase. A wine carafe. The syringe has glass facets like diamonds. Inside this glass is a sea. Deliverance is a spasm of violet lightning, a neon pulse, and how I am floating and not drowning. This is where I thought the river went and I was right.

"What bracelet?" Diego asks, mildly interested. He must cast me out to sea early tonight. He is dressed for dinner. How black his shoes are. Shoes to tango in. They would match a woman trimmed in sable.

"The diamond, at Christmas, in San Francisco. I threw it in the ocean," I say. I am smiling.

"You're hallucinating," Diego replies. "You take too much morphine."

"You can't take too much morphine," I laugh, my sailor and cigarette rasp they will remember. My delicacies will be lost. We are an assemblage of haphazard approximations. Then air eats the edges, salt water leaks in. Only the obvious and literal remain. We are headlines of events that did not quite occur. And bones and steel girders, teeth and locomotives, electric factories. But the squinting through sun on a ferry once, other vessels like paper boats, this too defined you, and will also be gone.

"Too much morphine," Diego says again. He's rushed now, gestures to Nurse.

Morphine is azure as southern harbors in summer, when they catch the great fish that have succumbed to hypnosis and slowed, let themselves drift. There are astonishments in such glassy seas. Women with sixty-seven nails in their flesh. Women who spend decades under blankets decorated with planets while their breath rises from their mouths in clouds of chickens and sausage, feathers and oxcarts. Perhaps I painted this.

"Did I paint? Or just cross bodies of water by ferry?" I am interested.

"Go to sleep now," Diego says, in his be-a-good-little-girl

voice, in the tone that hints at retribution. His priest voice, his teacher voice. "Sort through your tragedies. Put them in alphabetical order. Polish your scars. You are your own burn ward."

Ah, another Diego lie. Good Nurse. I am home, in my bedroom in the Casa Azul. I am in my wood canopied bed. My dolls on the shelves. Ribbons for my hair, silk flowers, hand-printed poems inside origami that a surrealist architect gave me as an act of love. I had asked him to set his house on fire as proof. I was disappointed. But I fucked him anyway, in a car parked on a boulevard, people passing inches away, carrying breads. My tokens, my trinkets. Miniature porcelain bowls. Soaps and lotions from China. Stone carvings of the deities of antiquity, giving birth and getting drunk. Quetzalcoatl, mentor of infidelity, patron of divorce, adored of women with one leg who crave morphine.

I could paint Diego with my eyes closed, without arms. Diego's voice is a tired intrigue. There is someone else for him to see tonight, a dancer he met in a cafe near a museum or gallery. Or the bohemian wife of an assistant. A woman in the walking coma of her eighth year of marriage who suddenly thinks, this is not matrimony. This is a felony. It should be outlawed. Now she wants to sit on Diego's lap, pretend he is Daddy and she is a bad girl. He will take her panties off and spank her. Pobrecito. So many women, so few routines.

Diego lingers, gone the restlessness. He brushes hair from my forehead. Each individual strand aches. Thirty thousand blades choreographed across my scalp. There is no urgency in his desire to leave me. Diego lets me know it isn't a passion. Tonight is an out-line, almost a mere conceptual infidelity.

There is no longer a thrill in betraying me. There is no sport left in it, not even for a man of Diego's redundancy. Now the excitement is abstract. He is able to make love while I die. He proves his separateness from me. I will be ash. He will live.

I would hold my diamond bracelet under candlelight. A green asserted itself from the edges like a subterranean forest. Within was a region of bridges and women wearing their grandmothers' heir-looms. A forest of women hiding melons and bits of green glass and bread. If I stared at the bracelet too long, I would go blind. That is why Diego gave it to me.

"I never gave you bourgeois diamonds. Sleep, Chiquita. Do you need another injection?" Diego sounds hopeful. His ace in the hole. He will play it now. It must be getting late. "Shall I call Nurse?"

I close my eyes. In the American winter, the trees looked raped. Diego said it was festive. It was the beginning of my solitary nights when I was illuminated by grace and vertigo.

I keep a syringe under my pillow now. I have one under the bed, and another taped in the hollow base of the night table lamp. Diego doesn't know I have bottles and syringes in the pottery and crystal vases, in drawers with my blouses, in my seashell and carved wood boxes containing necklaces and earrings. I have syringes taped into my dolls, held in place by adhesive bandages.

I am a bad girl. I am giving myself my own communion. I am meeting the border guards on my terms. I am traveling without a visa or a passport. They removed my leg, sawed it off like a diseased tree branch, but I still live.

"Is it raining?" This is a blank Diego should be able to fill in. He glances out the window.

"Not yet. But clouds are coming. It will rain by midnight," Diego says, making it a pronouncement.

"Until midnight then," I offer, and keep my eyes closed. I've seen enough anyway. Diego kisses my hand, touches my forehead as if testing for fever, and quietly removes himself from my room. The big man, enormous in his flesh, two hundred and sixty pounds of him, meat and wine and chocolates, and other women's mouths with their burgundy and vermilion lipsticks, with their jasmine and musk, their martinis and mink trim. Diego, scuttling away from a tiny woman who is inexorably turning into water.

Light rain just beyond the Zócalo on the bus back to Coyoacán. A corner. An intersection. Cuahutemotzin and Cinco de Mayo. The trolley car aimed itself at me and continued, a slow-motion archery, a ballet. It was loping. Then the trolley car pierced me. The collision of trolley car and bus. The pole. The twelve-foot pole impaled me. The metal handrail blasted through my pelvis, my uterus, shattering it. The metal handrail of the bus punched out my vagina. That was the point of exit. I lost my virginity then. I was raped by a machine that tried to kill me, and I have spent my life watching it do its work. Diego and I have observed it. I have curled into him, in the hollows of autumn, and wondered, as he slept, why so long? Why is this death taking so long? And why so little style?

The facts of my mutilation are public fodder. The details of my trolley car collision are better known than my paintings. Strangers recite a litany of fractures, abrasions, dislocations, battered organs, but they have not seen a single canvas. How can they know I painted not only the outline of my fate, but also the delicacies of its intention? External events have a psychology, a set of motivations. It is not a random universe.

I was fucked by a shaft of metal. In the accident, I was skewered on the handrail of the bus. It chose me. The force of impact tore my clothes off. I was singled out and taken from my region to another. There are vortices where pathways suddenly connect. Short circuits. An assembly of subterranean fires. And if you are there, you will die or be permanently altered.

I did not die. I thought of a desert at night lit by a sequence of small fires. My blood was hot. I thought someone was pouring coffee on me. I would have him arrested.

A nearby passenger had been holding a bag of gold powder. It was, after all, a fiesta day. It was a national celebration. It was a day when death wakes up, takes a shot of tequila, goes out stalking. Gold dust. The collision wrenched it from his hands and now the gold was falling on me, sticking to my blood, enhancing and changing it. It was a metamorphosis and I was already in transition. I was that day's ritual virgin.

Policemen. Firemen. A man with a pool cue, cigar, straw hat. Boys on bicycles. A little girl in pink ballet leotard. Her mother pulled her along, said, "Don't look there, Sweetie. It'll make you sick."

Then doctors arrived, made two groups of the injured, those who could be treated and those who would die. Or perhaps it was the Red Cross. I had been carried to a pool hall across the boulevard. I was not yet a whore with a sailor's mouth, arms a weave of puncture holes from morphine. I lay bleeding on green felt. I thought about chance. And the expression risking your life, betting everything. Perhaps they would continue to hit the hard balls with their sticks dipped in chalk, and maybe they did, through my blood, a thrilling new spin.

Doctors deposited me outside, on the boulevard, on cobblestones, with those too mutilated to survive. I had fractures of my spine, of my third and fourth lumbar vertebrae. I had pelvic fractures and a fracture of my right foot. My left elbow and shoulder were dislocated. The metal rod had made an abdominal wound as it entered through my left hip and forced its way out through my vagina. I had two crushed ribs. My right leg was broken in sixteen separate places.

But those are the obvious injuries. Such a list does not describe the fragile organs and tissues, the body beneath bones, where we keep our journals and kisses, our barricades and rafts.
The sky was as it is above oceans, an intensity of sheered turquoise imprinted by birds and clouds. That is what opened for me when my body was crushed. The ocean wind blew in. I became a harbor.

I was naked on the pool table. I had fantastic internal injuries. I was drizzled with bits of gold. My first boyfriend was with me. Alejandro. The name of the first boyfriend is like a tattoo engraved in a blackout. Alejandro, a good boy. He made doctors take me to the hospital with the ones who could be treated. They refused. Of course they wanted to let the beautiful ones live. It goes without saying, so no one dares to say it. Thin blondes. Redheads with sprinkles of freckles like nutmeg on their cheeks.

Alejandro argued with them. He explained that I attended the university. He made his voice fierce. He said my father was European and rich. Hungarian, my boyfriend Alejandro said. He did not say Jewish.

I was shivering and completely lucid. I realized they intended to leave me to die on the cobblestones, near the bus and trolley car collision. Near the disaster. Seven people died. I died, too, but unofficially.

"What's the point?" the first doctor asked. "Even if she lives, which she won't, she'll never have children."

The pragmatist. So I already offended their aesthetics and hierarchies, made their watches run backward, made nurses vomit. My name was barren bitch, abomination. But Alejandro made them carry my stretcher to an ambulance. I realized that our lives are not static, passive, but rather a dance. It is not enough that you choose it. It must also choose you. I have spoken with distinguished painters, sculptors, and actors who do not know this simple fact.

I possessed rare clarity. My body was a devastation. I had paid a blood price and something would be given in return. I would insist. My female possibilities were on a fiesta afternoon spilled onto the boulevard and pool hall floor. My eggs, with microscopic forests and stars and dramas gouged out. Gone, the way you scoop seeds from a melon.

There would be an exchange. I would be remarkable, haunting. I would negotiate. The score would be evened.

I was in the hospital for six months. The Red Cross Hospital on Calle Marta Ortega. There I had the first of the succession of plaster and metal casts that I have worn for thirty years. The prototype corset. Voodoo cast. Acts of malicious camouflage. I have measured my seasons by casts and surgeries, by the shifts of nurses, by highways of corridors tainted the yellow of fever and infection. The flutter of the nurses, snapping compacts shut, now sweaters across shoulders, clatter and laughter, the release into moonlight. That, and my increasing web of afflictions.

In the hospital, they didn't know what to do with my body, with my spine crushed like powder. Perhaps it would have been different if I were prettier. That's why I later began to wear gardenias and silk ribbons in my hair, Tehuana costumes, rebozos. It was Diego's idea. He created my unique appearance, what he called my look. He collected jewelry made in jungles from wood and stone and tin. And amulets, seed necklaces and strung pebbles with the sheen and serenity of jade. I was his doll to dress.

I learned how to decorate my face. Diego had a woman from

Hollywood, California, teach me to circle my eyes with kohl, outline my lips with magenta. She had a round suitcase like a leather hatbox filled with rouges and lipsticks. Diego said it was a method for survival. This was before he spoke of trademarks.

Morning was an intimacy. The chance survivors of cataclysm recognize the significance of gesture and ceremony. We know when to smile or cry. Later, I assembled my garments with the precision of a matador.

With enough tequila, it was always Day of the Dead. I was drunk, flagrant, glittering with bracelets and tragedy. It was the strategy of a terrified bitch in a region where buildings and plazas and fields have been leveled, eradicated. I ate corpses. I ate insects. I gnawed bark from trees. I ate dirt. Then I ate my leg.

The first cast, what they called without playfulness or irony a corset, yes. I was layered with wet strips of gluey fabric like a mummy, like a ghastly collage. I couldn't breathe. I thought they were suffocating me because I could no longer excite them with my pelvis, procreate, bear sons. They were hanging me from my head for nineteen hours. They were applying hot air to the cast, and it still didn't dry properly.

"Chiquita. You take all this too seriously," Diego would say, voice soft, glancing over his shoulder quickly, as if someone might overhear. "It's a three-ring circus. We sell our sisters for a chicken. Why are you surprised?"

It is winter. Diego reminds me of bread and soup and wood, feather down and wet hair. Diego is a confederation of grays, wool and flannel. A cooking fire. Thunder in another valley. This has nothing to do with us. It is a further Diego. It is after the hospitals and before we devised our trademarks.

Outside the Red Cross Hospital, in the courtyard below, by the fountain where the Alley of Orchids intersects the Alley of Angels, a beautiful woman with strong arms and a sundress spits into stagnant water. A man with a beard sits with a newspaper he isn't reading. A boy launches a paper boat. Birds. Stray sun. When I scream they give me morphine.

Then I am sent home to a room I cannot walk from. I will be encased in plaster for more than a year. I curse. I mimic crows. My voice coarsens. My throat feels metallic. No woman or dog could howl as I did, like a thing strangling on razored garbage.

I am half asleep on pills, no more injections. It is my bedroom in my parent's house, where I was born, the Casa Azul, with its walls like languid iris. Then I understood. The methods for my unbreaking had yet to be invented. They should have left me with the untreatables. I was already living posthumously. Then I began painting.

I knew the border where absence is an ache, sunlight a betrayal. I recognized the raw scalloped edges, the deceptive taint in bone and leaf, shaky midnight, an interminable violation. Only a woman who has already died could dare to paint as a woman. A dead woman would use her stumps and the textures of terra cotta, the creamy mucus of afterbirth.

A dead woman would know the sky turns thin and tinny when wind blows through the bleached rags of banners strung above a squalid bazaar. Shadows fall on hungry women searching for shoes, any two that match. Residues linger on boulevards and become part of the air, a necessary element, like clouds and ports and nightmares.

I would begin with Frida. The one with the limp and rum, waiting for the lie of a healed scar and amnesia. I would study her face in mirrors in rooms where there were none. In the glass that wasn't there.

I did not feel like a victim from this accident. I felt chosen. Strangely, the actual collision was a clarification. I suspected that I was inexorably different. But an intuition is not proof. Now I had conviction.

Paradoxes ran through me like parallel rivers. My Catholic mother, hard, stiff, and black in her certainties, in her burrow bordered by rosaries and saints, by the perpetuation of generations of rumors of implausible deeds. The tropics made the European version vivid and inflamed.

My Jewish father, with the Europe he had run from like a charcoal stain behind him, indifferent to his traditions, which he rejected. My father with platforms and train stations perched on his shoulders behind him. And the massive edifices of gray stones, buildings, courtyards, and cities, all was a gritty smoke as he abandoned them. This was my original heritage. I was severed from the source. I had not yet constructed bridges and fashioned ports where there are none.

In my first solitary confinement, in my exile, I felt my other contradictory impulses. The female and antifemale parts of me, separate rivers, also parallel. I saw this in my face, when I tied back my hair and wore a man's hat and suit. I could be a man, handsome, virile. A good drinker, bourbon and gin. A man who studied mathematics and went to brothels. I could make any girl love me, remember my cigar, how I was good with a knife. I had so many faces already. I was why you shouldn't cross oceans, forget the names of your ancestors and the reasons for their journeys, but you do.

The accident was a clarity. I was freed. How mediocre I would have been without this chance event. In the months of incapacity, my true nature emerged. I was a solitary. No rules applied to me.

I accepted this. I relished it. Some women are born criminals. It's a calling, like the cloth or politics. A certain sensibility. A kind of music. You are born with this renegade capacity. Some women have an ability to differentiate the strata of night. They are geologists of darkness. Often, such women are burned at the stake or confined to lunatic asylums.

I had polio when I was six. I was signaled out. My right leg withered. They said it would heal and I knew they were lying. It was in the Casa Azul in Coyoacán. I should have been more attentive to this singularity. It was the first time the larger hand touched me. It was an unexpected flame, a slap from a stranger. I did not heal completely, would have to camouflage my right leg, the pathetic one, always. That and the two distinct bloodlines running alongside each other like American highways, straight and uncluttered, almost unborn. In California with Diego, the actor Edward G. Robinson gave us his Cadillac. We would drive the enormous red car without a roof sixty and seventy miles an hour all day but the two roads did not meet.

Some women are solitaries. People are, for them, an acquired taste. Some women are riding a bus with their boyfriend when they are fucked with a twelve-foot metal rod. The conductor yanked it out. He said, I must pull this out now or she will die. I heard the crack of my bones like a woman making cakes does, breaking one egg after another, eggs on the rim of a glass bowl, eggs on the rim of a glass bowl, and the chain stops.

I knew the eerie spawn of rivers in mist. I was sensitive. I was the product of a chemical and electrical intelligence I would paint. I would explore my many faces in the multiple incarnations I already simultaneously led.

I had a vast capacity for absence and silence. I knew borders meet only because we say they do. They meet from consensus. Ask Diego on the scaffolds, with his carpenters and patrons, his architects, the men and women who serve his ambition with measuring devices, equations and instruments to divide and project angles. Diego thinks he has the proof. He is wrong.

Diego considers a field and sees sunflowers and the backs of women. He has a vision of women gathering calla lilies, holding them in their arms like children or swans. Women with braids, on their knees in dirt. He prefers their backs because then they are like cattle or piñon trees. He does not consider their faces, which might require thought. Diego's women are merely symbols, leached of meaning. He might as well be reciting the Communist Manifesto or prayers with a rosary. Poor Diego. If the earth opened any further for him, he would collapse beneath its unexpected possibilities, its bold dimensions you cannot find on a blueprint.

I examine a field and see the ocean on the afternoon of resurrection, when the polio and plague, consumption and accident dead open their coffins, sit up slowly, dumbly, and are washed in water of larkspur and delphiniums.

I have arms like this, embossed with eagles and iris and silver roses. I have hidden the names of lovers, etched them in lost languages even a bruja could not decode. I have gray pearl teeth. You have a boat. We will cross an ocean. We will leave no trace, no artifact, not even the soft rustle of autumn leaves, spreading their virulent rumors.

"You are wild with your imagination," Diego is saying. "You're stealing Demerol and morphine. Do you crawl like a snake to get it? Anyway, I'm going to lock it up."

"I will jump out the window," I say. This is an idle threat. I have more bottles hidden. Hundreds of glass vials.

Diego smokes and does not offer me a cigarette. It might be raining.

"I want a cigarette," I tell him.

"I am afraid of Nurse," Diego admits. "She will report me. You're coughing blood."

"Fuck you, coward. I am dying and you think of being compromised?" I spit at him. A patch like rust forms on his shirt. "You sicken me. Leave." And Diego is gone.

I limp on crutches to the window. I have one leg and too many faces. Why is death taking so long? Rain today. Another morning. Of course, sailors know the meaning of such rain, its devious promise. The harbors seem derelict, abandoned. Gulfs of contagion where you do not expect them, beneath the ship, on your hands. A sudden reef not noted on the charts. A rock the size of a cathedral no one has ever seen before, a volcanic rock at night and no lighthouse.

From the window of the veranda, everything is lime and chartreuse, even the cactus are greened. It is the forest at the beginning, the archetypal pattern, palm trees and ferns. And beneath their fronds, something crawling on its belly, something hungry, evolving teeth. I howl until my throat is hoarse and I begin coughing.

Diego gives me back the key to the medicine cabinet. "Crawl to it, then," he says, half a whisper, harsh. He wants me dead. I am dead. I laugh a long time.

It's a laugh they will call my pulque laugh, my drunk-on-tequila-and-Demerol sailor laugh. My lover of women laugh. They will say Frida was a bad boy. She wore a Panama hat and boots. You could hear her at a fiesta, throat raw from marijuana and cigarettes. And it is true. I howled in my solitary nights, my gray wolf nights, my woman of the harbor without a lighthouse nights.

I know the amber of streetlights in hotels in cities where your unfaithful husband has left you for five consecutive nights in the honeymoon suite. Lamplight leaks in. This is how you get infection and cancer. This is how you discover genius and disaster. Then he returns, bathes, pretends you know nothing, suspect nothing. Five minutes. Five nights. Am I not to have noticed the difference?

"Move," Diego commands. I refuse.

Diego grabs my tequila bottle. It disappears. Then the long skirt to camouflage the cripple. He carries me to the shower and deposits me there. Then he carries me to the hotel bed. Later, on his knees, he dresses me as he would an only child. Then he trots me out, clothed in ritual costume. Diego is my partner. We must meet the new men with the new money.

"I'm a bad boy," I tell Diego and laugh.

"I know." Diego stands near the chauffeur. I slide into the limousine like a trained dog.

"Love is like arson. It's lethal," I say. Diego returns the tequila bottle.

"You're so festive," the wife of a potential patron in some American city says, delighted. "What alegría." She demonstrates her Spanish.

A mahogany table with silver candelabras and a vase with enormous roses each threaded to an individual wire, each a separate crucifixion. They are in pain. It is obvious. That is what gives them flush and ambiance. Or are they in traction?

"Dying is a gift," I say. "You must practice constantly. Like the violin." I refuse to look at the flowers in their wretchedness.

Laughter. That is Frida, Diego's crippled wife. Frida, his trained monkey. They say she fucks sailors and schoolgirls. Diego and Frida. What an exceptional marriage. They're the new frontier. A completely modern union. I would close my eyes and think, this is how barbarians lived. There is nothing new about it.

The polio. Then the banishment to plaster and metal. Was I expected to heal my injuries, simply by being imprisoned in layers of gauze that turned rock hard? Were they indifferent? Perhaps they lit candles. They did card tricks. They pulled straws. Perhaps, in the hospital plaza, they sacrificed goats or chickens, read tea leaves, made an augury of a drowned woman's intestines.

Where is Diego? Has he gone back to Italy? Has he taken a woman to the theater, to talk about Chicago and Trotsky and the possibilities for cubism in cinema? Then I want Nurse. Nurse or I will scream.

There was an exchange. I gave them my human body, my standard-issue female possibilities, and in return, they let me open the door. I traded my body for canvas. I bartered human love for a palette, for having the veil removed from my eyes. There had been a trade, and I got the better of it.

I was seventeen. I was encased in plaster for an entire year. I could not walk or sit. I was discovering my extraordinary proclivities. It was as if I had been sent to a convent in disgrace and actually found faith. But this was better. My fingers were lilies and scalpels, my hands fragrant metals.

I began my first paintings, lying on my back, with an easel fixed across my chest and the ceiling for inspiration. I would develop my third eye. I would know dusks are disguised, a mime of shadowed iris and asters. Painters and madwomen know this. Angry women. Discarded women. Women who lose their symmetry. Women who will not conform.

Perhaps I yearned for Alejandro. He was a reference point. He saved my life. Early autumn. I craved the sound of water, it eased my sleep. I desired water like a woman with a pathological thirst. It was a seductive lantern-yellow autumn, promising danger and revelation.

Alejandro had been sent abroad. He was a coward. He went. His mother did not want him to marry a woman who might be dying, who could not bear children. I was already a woman of suspicion and rumor. I was already a woman you must speak of in whispers.

October was a treachery. Alejandro's letters were less frequent. It was said he was near Barcelona, in a small villa on the Mediterranean. Inside my cast, I shrugged. Autumn is the season of uncertain navigation. The wives of fishermen in mourning know this. They stand below cliffs where ships come and go with cargoes of orphans and mangoes. Such currents contain artifacts, femurs and lilacs. Nothing is sunken or lost. It is merely temporally misplaced. It will return while you stand undone by stars and just as naked, waiting. I will hand it to you. I am the sailor. I am the girl.

The autumn of my seventeenth year was a vast interior ocean. The garden beyond the veranda floated. Dusk was wave break and dog bark, thunder, stone. The crisp snap of a woman hit on the mouth by a drunk man. The almost imperceptible sound of her lip as it begins to swell.

I dreamt each night of the accident. The utter silence in the seconds before the collision of the bus and trolley car. Sounds of bones breaking like your feet make when you cross a desert playa, how the salty white sand cracks beneath your sandals like so many insect wings. Then you know wind is composed of a legion of tiny things that are being extinguished.

My younger sister, Cristina, told me Alejandro was now engaged. October of the severing, roots blown off. A pause, then earthquakes, bankruptcy, broken engagements. Not a garden outside but patches of old leather. Between brittle grasses are coffins of bleached pine.

Midnight trees rustling russet and umber. They answer to the moon. Gravity. Immutable laws of how things spin and remain in air. The moon thinned like a woman with tuberculosis. It was a flinty antique ivory above the veranda and the garden with its carcasses of sunflowers. Suffocated moon picked raw.

"I don't believe you don't care," my sister Cristina said.

"I feel spared," I told her. Rhythm of paint and brush was a form of music.

Then night went into remission. A new cycle. There were noons when I drowned in clarity, sky so fierce and unflawed it made my face ache. My eyes wanted to fall out. I had to hold them back with the pressure of my fingers. "You can't blame Alejandro," Cristina pointed out.

"I don't blame him," I said. Soon would come the somber hour of cathedral bells plying their trade through rain. Cristina's babble was taking the last of the light.

"Mother knows you don't pray," Cristina tried.

"Go to hell," I said. "Put a sharp stick up your ass and go to the hot place."

"What should I tell Mother?" Cristina asked, daring me. Her face reddened. She wanted more.

"Tell her to accompany you," I suggested.

Ordinary women are trivial, with their ghastly repetitions and the ordeal of tradition. Monotone women, in Spanish and German, Russian and Chinese, discussing the prices of blouses and oranges and where the buses go, where the men and children go.

"Mother says you're healing," Cristina said.

"It's her most convenient explanation. And I consigned you to flames," I responded. "Go, or I'll give you stomach cancer."

Early winter. Now the cathedral bells were brassy, like horns, a blown shell, and some reprobate indigenous element asserting itself. There was a constant clash in the air and a sense of the day being sliced.

My sisters brought me a bouquet each afternoon and a special arrangement on religious occasions. They wore velvet and jackets trimmed with red silk. When other women evaluated their party gowns, I would instead contemplate a cool set of cutting blades. That would be my fiesta season. There is something celebratory in metal so thin and sharp your flesh begs for its touch. If you loved me, you would kiss me with steel. You would give me more than twelve long-stemmed roses twisted onto wire. You would carve my entire name in your chest.

My younger sister carried flowers to me. It was one of her domestic tasks and the tenseness in her jaw told me she resented this. The visitation with the suspected-to-be-mad-and-deviant sister. The asymmetrical one dying or malingering. Cristina was the one they dispatched to demonstrate they had not forgotten me. Frida, in the metaphorical attic where such relatives are traditionally kept.

On Christmas Mother climbed the stairs to my room. She stood near the window on a day the texture of cold adobe. Her face was partial in the extravagant light. Her face looked leached, absorbed, rubbed away. Noon. The air burned and glared.

My mother was trapped in black, neck to wrist to toe. My mother looked strangled in her uniform against sin. She was alert. She could detect aberration in the air, the way some women have an allergy to certain flowers or scents.

Afternoon turned brutal, feral. I lived in her house but we rarely spoke. I had to translate my thoughts to fit her remedial conceptions. Her version of events was bead size. I was going to hell. She had her rudimentary intuitions. And the gossip of neighbors.

"It's Christmas," my mother informed me, not with her mouth

but through her corsets and saints' beads and absolute assurances. There were saints she knew by name who helped you find lost goats, and took away bad lungs. Saints who protected you from bandits and poison. "Put out your cigarette, please."

She did not ask how I was. My physical condition was avoided like floor washing and pot scouring, a task left for the maids. I was an obligation she wished left for someone else. I put out my cigarette. I kept my bottle of brandy under the pillow.

My mother presented me an opal ring. It seemed an afterthought, wrapped in a lace handkerchief, extracted from a stiff skirt pocket. I wore men's suits and refused to put powder on the hairs above my lips. I blasphemed and refused to go to church. I was a heretic, receding from her, becoming less identifiable. Perhaps I hadn't come from her womb after all. Was it the Jew's fault? Hadn't she suspected?

"You'll never have babies. Who will marry you?" My mother did not expect an answer. "You're no good for the convent. Hobbies, I suppose. Painting. Swimming. When the cast comes off, they say you could swim. Even with your deformity."

"I swim as I move from one side of the bed to the other," I said. "I have entire underwater weeks."

"Then swimming it is," my mother concluded, touching her rosary beads, almost fondling them. These were her perfect children. There was nothing malformed around her neck.

I am injecting Demerol into my arm. Day and no Diego. Cristina lets me have Demerol. It is better than morphine. I have embroidered my arms from my fingers to my elbow with an inked calligraphy. Some women stitch rugs. I have created a tapestry on my skin. I can't find the veins within all that forest and moss. I shut my eyes and my hands guide me to the source, the river inside. This is how you navigate and weave after you go blind.

"That never happened," Cristina says.

It is afternoon and my sister visits me. I tell her about the opal Christmas gift and she says, "You're making a fantasy."

I find a vein in my wrist. I breathe in violets, subtle, delicate, just rained on. You could not gather this and put it in a bottle and sell it for perfume. It would be too costly. And my lungs are miniature roses, small like fish mouths.

"It's your birthday in a few days," Cristina says, invitational. "What do you want?"

"Demerol." I think I am speaking.

"The drugs are driving you crazy. You're telling lies about Mother again." Cristina almost scolds me.

Eventually, our mothers become sketches. They recede behind our shoulders in their contrived finery, in their fraudulence and piety, their invented aristocracy, their pathetic postures they thought glamorous. Stolen. Our mothers, who wear our mouths and eyes. They are behind us like smoke. Women without a sense of orchestration. Such women are bad liars. When they abandon you, they let it show. They do not bother to pretend. They do not hide their tracks.

"Mother adored you," Cristina is saying. It is raining. Rivers are falling against stone walls. This is how moss and gorges are formed. It's continuous. It does not require love.

It is summer. My arm is a meadow of wild flowers and our mothers are becoming sketches, charcoal smudges fading behind us, taking with them the absurd tragedies that we believed.

"I believed everything," I tell Cristina.

"What? About Mother?" Cristina is startled.

"Mother is a fraud," I say.

"You say that about everyone," my sister answers, avoiding my face.

The forest like the heart is outlined in neon. It's not an organ but a peninsula with harbors and spice markets, wind chimes. If it is summer, the women on the boulevards are bare armed, skin distilled almond. Sundresses. Jasmine perfumes. Eyes like ceramic beads. They are fertile. You smell when they bleed.

Cristina pours herself rum, drinks it quickly, like a medicine. Cristina is drinking amber rain. It has drifted across cobblestones where teenagers are left to die.

"I won't be a lie to my daughter," I reveal. "I tell my Flora everything. There are no awkward gestures. She brings me Demerol when Nurse is sleeping."

"You've been a wonderful mother," Cristina offers. Pause. "You are exceptional."

I do not pretend to be already resolved, as if adulthood were a state of perpetual grace. My daughter understands me as a work in progress, deceived by circumstance, confused by complexity. Morning is a moral choice, to lace up the shoes, if you have shoes, to let the sun graze your cheeks, to continue to accommodate the cathedral bells, to take the taunt of boulevards, stones stained like eroding tin. We step on our amulets. We can say yes or no.

"You are a gifted mother, of course," Cristina says. I have exhausted her.

I ask for cigarettes and tequila. Cristina agrees. I'm surprised. "No lectures?"

"It's nearly your birthday." Cristina smiles.

We exist in isolation, lanterns in our lungs. That's what creates our light, its magnitude and gravity. The contagious latitudes, where women with wounds watch the salt wash in. Women treading withered legs through red kelp.

I began to paint when I was seventeen. I was incarcerated in my bedroom at the Casa Azul. There was a queer yellow light that summer. It accentuated the stains and residues. That was when the moon had the sheen of dog teeth. It turned the sky to sand, a powder like crushed spine. That year the harvest should have been condemned.

I walked, finally, took the bus, the trolley car. I thought I was cured. The street accepted me as it would a stray leaf. I returned to the university. I had no conviction for anything but painting and committing acts of outrage. I dressed like a man. I flirted with women in bookstores. To a clerk reading poetry near the window I said, I'd go to jail for a mouth like yours. I took her to a bohemian hotel. I insisted she keep the gaudy light on. Touch that lamp and I'll break your wrist, I said. I made her cry. I refused to tell her my name and left her alone at 4 A.M.

My mouth devised profanities, effortlessly, as if I wasn't even there. I smoked cigarettes and marijuana. I wore a man's gold watch on a chain. I carried a bottle of brandy in my jacket pocket. It was how I spit on their plazas and universities, their hospitals and bureaucracy. It was sabotage. It was like starting a multitude of invisible fires. It was a way of keeping warm in my expanding solitude.

I was reckless and angry. I wandered boulevards in the after-midnight darkness, drunk. Twice I slept the night in churches. I woke up in parks. Sometimes I walked down streets screaming.

My philosophy professor took me to his apartment. We made love. Then I asked if he had friends who could join us. My professor went to a café, returned with his two cousins. I want you to watch, I told my professor. I poured him a glass of brandy. I lit his cigar. I arranged the chair where I wanted him to sit, the light and angle. He sat and watched. When I left I said, You do not exist. Never approach me again. Then in an alley, I fell to my knees and wept.

The revolution was a hazy flutter on the periphery. Viva Marx. Viva Lenin. And the air was vivid, cinnamon and copper, a seduction into possibility. Perhaps the revolution would bring a new way to dance. Something faster than a tango, more complicated and dangerous. A dance you might need a password for. Or a dance enacted near a precipice. You could have more to worry about than a rose thorn on your tongue.

The revolution was the agitated floral wallpaper in the lobby of a cheap hotel. It was vases of poppies and window boxes of moist geraniums made vague by dust. The revolution was bougainvillea and hibiscus, blooms hanging like nests of lamps. I thought of belladonna. I thought of illumination. I thought of being scalded. I felt hot and watched. The revolution was wild red bells. Everything was music. Speeches punctuated by horns and drums, clapping and foot stamping. The horizon was crepe paper that swayed. I walked with a slight limp. I felt festive.

Then the wind parted and Diego was there. He just appeared. That was his way. Commissions were presented like offerings, and he was there, with his scaffolds and brushes, followers and whores, carpenters and assistants with their mistresses and wives, their girlfriends from the provinces. And there were architects and patrons, mayors and judges, the curious, the spectators, the flamboyant, the desperate, the whole sickening horde that Diego called humanity, the workers, and brothers.

I considered Zapata and his camp followers. I thought, so this is Diego Rivera and his sideshow. It was nothing like Zapata. No one in Diego's camp looked hungry. No one was firing pistols at them. I was disappointed. In the vacant place where my painting would someday live, I was shocked.

Later, I realized that it was Diego who made me distrust magic. Why think it will be a rabbit or dove coming out of a hat? It might be a baby monster.

I thought, he is hideous. In that clarified late afternoon light I realized that fame is a form of beauty. It's what you cannot buy. It alters what is being seen. Diego, monumental rather than excessive. The artist as what we are manipulated to interpret. Diego Rivera, substantial rather than grotesque. His celebrity caused a rearrangement in perception itself, in the atoms composing rooms and the molecules of your eyes.

I brought lunches to the scaffolds where Diego was working. I spent entire mornings devising and assembling lunches in woven baskets I decorated with flowers, fronds, stones. I combined textures and spices. It was a child's sorcery. I wooed him with hibiscus braided into a bamboo basket containing stuffed peppers and apples. Chicken breasts with lemon required yellow orchids. With breads, I used straw and cassia and daffodils as my base. I found a market where a woman sold irises so purple they looked black. I moistened them with my spit, made them darker, placed them between chocolates.

Finally, Diego spoke to me. He contrived to see me alone, after the others, even the lingerers, had left the scaffolds. I had been patient. The sun was beginning to set like certain satins and curry.

"Do you wish to see my gun?" Diego asked. He produced his silver-plated pistol and spun it in a circle with his extraordinary fat fingers. "Again?" he asked, hopeful, enthusiastic.

"No," I declined. "Everyone has seen your gun. It's contrived."

"You're flat like a boy," Diego said, evaluating my body. "You could be a boy. I like that."

That day I wore a necklace of crude bronze dogs inspired by the graves of Colima. It was by chance, though I believe nothing is purely accidental. Afternoon was winding down, and I had draped a woven rebozo around my shoulders. It formed an unexpected composition of strands.

Diego reached out to my chest, took my necklace in his hands and said, "Which are you? A boy or a dog?"

"When I'm on my knees, is there a difference?" I asked.

Diego was aware of the desirability of a consistently recognizable assistant, someone indigenous. That would play well in Moscow and New York. It had photographic promise. He was looking for an image that appealed. I chanced to be it. The girl to hold the magician's cape would be dark skinned, with a native costume. Diego was not searching, precisely, but he was alert. He wanted to be startled, shocked.

Wind was blowing, softly. It smelled, simultaneously, of desert and sea, sagebrush and spring onions. We were standing near the scaffolds, the boulevard beyond us. It must have been autumn, the trees were yellowing. There were conspiracies in the imported European sycamores and lindens. There was an amber intrigue in the chestnut branches. In an alternative version of events, I could read Diego's mind and I slapped his face, hard. I punched him as a man would and called him filthy. He trembled with pleasure and thanked me.

In this Mexico City, my mouth was a flagrant crimson like sails on pirate ships. My basket of strawberries was sun ruined on the cobblestones. I was hiding my polio-withered right leg, the one that was later severed by saw. Even then, I knew how to pose with my leg concealed. I had learned to make my eyes mimic onyx and night rivers. My intricate bead earrings cast shadows of birds across my neck and cheeks. It looked like it was raining hawks across my face. I could project my own climate. I said, "Well? Do you want me?"

"I want to give you a bath," Diego replied. "I'll pretend you're a street whore I picked up at a nightclub. I'll bathe you and call you by your new name."

"Just don't bore me," I said. I put out my cigarette and left the basket in the plaza.

Diego took me to a hotel he admired for its decadence and new black marble bathtubs imported from Italy. Diego said its opulence reminded him of whorehouses so legendary even he had not been there. This was one of his profound regrets. They had been outlawed and burned before he knew of them.

Hotel de la Noche Roja was located on an alley bordered by dynasties of bougainvillea along fences sheltering groomed lawns with tennis courts near the city. It was later destroyed by earthquake. But in the season of our courtship, it was where theater performers and drug smugglers went for illicit love. You took the wives of politicians to this hotel, ballerinas, girl and boy children. It was elegant and notorious. Everyone wore sunglasses and the staff pretended not to recognize you.

The walls were creamy brocade, the lampshades a pale gold. There were gold ovals embossed into the fabrics, and leaves with sharply serrated edges. I thought, that's how Diego will mutilate me, with a dull blade crowded with ridges. Then he instructed me to take off my clothing.

"Just stand there," Diego said. He had removed his shirt. He was sweating. "You're tiny. You're deformed. Your body is a tragedy," he noted, with delight. " I must know the origin of each trauma." He traced my stomach and thigh scars with a hand holding a cigarette. "Were you taken prisoner by the secret police? You are still in pain, yes?"

He was suddenly happy, lighter. He hummed a fashionable jazz. He was lathering me with a spice-scented soap. It might have been ginger. He produced a razor. "I'll shave you," Diego offered. "Like in a brothel."

"Where?" It was happening in slow motion, like the bus and trolley car collision. I stood where I was, fixed in place, while the trolley car kept coming, aiming for me. I did not move.

"Everywhere. All your hair," Diego replied. He poured a glass of champagne for me.

I stood naked in a huge pink marble bathtub. A breeze in leaves outside. I could sense them, and a desert wind that had recently brushed across magenta sand. It had been a chance occurrence which had both enhanced and infected it. Somewhere, the moon was stuck above a bay made vivid and brutal by an abnormal current. It was both a vessel and an anchor.

"Tell me about brothels," I said to Diego.

Diego was on his knees with a washing cloth, soap, and a razor. He paused. "You haven't worked in one?" He seemed surprised. "But you must. I will arrange it tomorrow."

"I am painting tomorrow," I replied. "So tell me now."

Diego told me. There was the initiation, examination, and alteration. Then the next level, the shaving of body hair, the washing, of course, and then one could proceed into the decoration. This varied with country and century. Diego preferred the harem concubines of odalisques, women smoking powders from enameled lacquer holders. Women holding pipes of hashish and opium, pipes called hookahs. Women stretched out on tapestry rugs and cushions, intoxicated. Such is the posture and facial expression of a permanent, unburdened yes. Their legs would be spread. Their arms would be rounded in a gesture of compliance, open, overtly invitational.

"You will pay attention to Renoir and Ingres," Diego said. "You will memorize the traditional combinations. Rings and veils. Clothing a fist can reach beneath. No buttons. Bare feet. Red mouth. Kohl eyes. Anklets."

"Scarves meant to be ripped off," I offered.

"Yes." Diego nodded his head. "Then I would paint your boy nipples fuchsia."

Diego reconsidered. In the brothel, the owner of the establishment would do it, he said. It would be more erotic to have another hand form the lather and razor me off. Diego would watch.

He would sit in a gold upholstered chair, holding his pistol and smoking a cigar. Now he was rinsing me with a fragrant mist, an oily summer perfume that reminded me of gardenias in too much abundance, like at someone's grandmother's funeral.

"Imagine what happens next," Diego said, drying me with a thick bath towel in which the leafy pattern of the walls was also ingrained. I am being embossed on the inside and outside. I am being made singular to the bone, I thought. My blood cells are being rearranged. This is how a painting should be, not merely canvas but to the marrow.

Diego was watching me. He had wrapped me in a towel. "Are you thinking about what happens next?" He asked. He lit a cigarette. It was a languid dusk.

I said yes. I thought of concubines and slaves, lounging on sofas and embroidered with sequin pillows, women arranged on their sides like offerings. They are taught to do this, to present themselves, to gesture with their eyes. I considered still lifes, a plate of pears and a vase of orange tiger lilies. That is how Diego likes his woman, I thought. They must be still as fruit, mere objects for the appetite, not so different from chocolates.

I assumed Diego would want me facing upward on the bed, with its brocade against my back. I was prepared for this, a further intimacy with the golden fibers. Instead, he turned me onto my belly. I was startled.

Diego laughed. "I am going to call you Pierre. Will you answer to that name? I like the French. Have you yet been to France?"

I said yes, I would answer to Pierre. And no, I had not yet been to France. Then I asked why he had positioned me on my stomach.

"You are too distorted to be a woman. You mock proportion. You are disgusting." Diego was studying my back, my legs. "You are the opposite of a miracle."

"I understand," I said. Perhaps I smiled.

"There are whorehouses in Marseilles where mothers bring their ten-year-olds in exchange for a dollop of heroin. I have seen this bartering made for one coin-size piece of opium. Take her, I have heard mothers say. Take this nine-year-old. I named her for a flower or a jewel. Rose or Sapphire. Mary or Ruby. But what's in a name, anyway?" Diego paused.

"I am Pierre," I said.

"That's the right answer. That is the only possible right answer. So I will continue with your lesson. I have heard the mothers say, see how thin she is, so completely flat-chested? You can use her as a boy. That should count extra. And notice the soft swell of her buttocks." Diego put out his cigarette. He was tracing a plump finger down my back as if preparing to paint a canvas. "So thin," he continued, "but she'll be surprisingly accommodating. My boyfriend swears by this one. He says he found god in her ass. He says she makes sounds like a sea mammal when you penetrate her from behind. She barks like a stranded seal and rolls and heaves like she was riding waves. Try her. She's better than sailing."

Diego was completely still. His fingers were poised on his gold belt buckle. He was standing near the bed. "What happens next?" he asked.

"I make certain you find god," I said, eyes closed.

This was my audition. When he was finished, when the evening had concluded itself, we smoked cigarettes and marijuana in the hotel room. We drank tequila later in a bar near a park. I told him about the trolley car accident and how I was utterly broken. Diego found this attractive. My withered leg with sixteen separate fractures. How I was impaled by metal. Then my solitary confinement, the corsets that kept air from my lungs.

"Tell me about the gold dust again," Diego closed his eyes. "Tell me again how you screamed louder than a siren or rabid dog. I want to make you scream like that."

"Of course you do," I said. "I insist."

Then Diego asked specific questions about procedures, length of operations, numbers of stitches. He asked about skin grafts and infections. He wanted to trace certain wounds with his tongue. I took my dress off my shoulders. It was a public park. An occasional couple passed. It was night, lamplit. Diego was wearing sunglasses and counting stitches with his tongue.

I closed my eyes. Diego wanted information on the wounds that he encountered with his mouth. I provided it. He smiled at my descriptions. I felt his mouth twist on my back, like a muted kiss. I felt his excitement. I thought of autumn women in their private burn wards. I did not reveal my capacity for evaluating October nights, how variations of amber, chartreuse, and lime opened for me like a text written by quill on parchment. I did not tell Diego I could glance across a patio and see eyes between stalks of Brazilian canna. Or how I perceived the city as it truly was, the rancid sheen, the feverish golds, how trees shivered. I was not blinded by lamplight. I could decipher intention. I could hear the city moan and beg for mercy through her twisted no-teeth mouth.

"You're certain you are temporary?" Diego repeated.

"Absolutely," I assured him. "I am degenerating. It's inevitable."

"What will you do?" Diego took off his sunglasses. "In between?"

"I will fuck and be fucked by strangers. I will go to museums and watch rivers and birds. I will drink and I will paint," I said.

"If we marry, will your routine be the same?" Diego stared at me.

"I will engage in acts of anarchy. Solitude. Art. Maybe I'll commit suicide." I was leaning on one elbow, on the grass in the park, studying his face, the loose flesh that was his neck.

"That's the right answer. Because I will walk out a door and have dinner in Moscow or Peking. I answer to no one. Maybe Rockefeller and Lenin. But not a crippled boy with a terminal and ludicrous infection." Diego stared at an area of my shoulder, discolored, scooped an inch deep, the abandoned ruin of a skin graft that refused. "You have flesh like a leper."

I thanked him. I considered marrying Diego. He would take me to seas from antiquity. The Arabian, Caspian, Ionian. The Sagasso, Adriatic, and Black. One could still find artifacts there, and enormous seashells, bigger than his hands. Species of fish believed extinct proliferate in such waters. The fishermen have boats of raw wood planks held together by leather. The boats are out now, in currents of lilac and bone.

"And the bruises? The mottling? You are certain it is permanent?" Diego was completely alert.

"Like tattoos. Don't be afraid. I am incurable and dying." We were passing tequila back and forth. And it was settled.

Our short courtship, a few camellias and white jasmine by lamplight. Perhaps we spoke of painting, his and mine, Kandinsky and Monet, Renoir and Degas. Perhaps we spoke of world events and made a list of politicians we wished dead. October and then November women walked along boulevards in navy wool, silk scarves at their throats and high leather gloves. Such women change their names with each affair, the way married women rotate linen. Such women have imported purses that rattle with vials of scent, brochures describing villas in African colonies where they do not intend to go. Their purses contain postcards from cities not visited.

Diego and I at one café or another. Around us, autumn women were passing, their woolen suits smelling like cloves. They take better care of their closets than their children, I thought and told Diego. I knew more. How such women wore glass rings they swore were rubies. And such women knew of remedies in alleys and exchanges under night bridges.

There was the matter of my father's mortgage on the Casa Azul. Diego wrote a check for this. One check and it was done.

It occurred to me that some women fall in love with a season, a month, like October or November. The man is incidental to the process, a mere catalyst. If a woman forgot this, she might find herself remaining indoors, wearing dark taffeta with complicated skirts, trailing through rooms like a captured raven. That is what happened to Mother, her feathers stern, glistening as if oiled. Clipped completely. Bathed in tar. But it would not happen to me. I was Pierre, after all.

"Do you remember the Hotel de la Noche Roja?" I ask Diego.

Cristina has left. She has gone to buy me a birthday gift. Little bells from Oaxaca. Diego has reappeared. Perhaps they come in shifts now, to watch me constantly. They do this with condemned prisoners when they suspect suicide. Now Diego smiles, says yes. "That is where you first bathed me." Diego says.

"Why would I bathe you?" I ask. My mouth feels blistered, metallic.

"You gave me baths for years. To wash off the residues of the scaffolds. The paints and turpentine. The city traffic. You wore a red kimono with a pattern of red dragons. You were my concubine. Then you rubbed me with almond oil." Diego is not looking at me.

"I don't remember it that way," I tell him. "You called me Pierre."

"You were dressed like a man. Even your shoes. You were aggressive. You demanded I treat you like a sailor," Diego says. "You wanted to be slapped. Those were your conditions."

"You said we could make marriage a form of war," I accuse.

"An epic of debasement," Diego clarifies.

"An international scandal," I say.

"Something to feed the hyenas with cameras," Diego agrees.

"You loved the cameras," I remember.

"As you did." Diego is watching the smoke from his cigar. "It's a paradox."

We laugh with our entire mouths, gulping air. We hold hands. We are happy. I smoke. It is raining. The city is an assemblage of weedy indigo ruins. On the ocean floor, apple and citrus orchards are lightly rooted in sand. And rows of gutted cornflowers. On salty boulevards drowned goats and trees you cannot use for firewood.

"You hurt me in the hotel room," I remind him. "You made me retch."

"All your memories are hideous," Diego says.

"I need Demerol," I say.

"How many bottles do you have hidden?" he asks.

"Almost a thousand," I lie. I have more than that. I have boxes that contain two hundred bottles. I have more than five of these boxes. And so many separate vials, stuck in crevices of my room, taped and glued inside and behind objects, sewn into clothing.

"You slither to the floor, Frida? You crawl on your belly to find them? You count them one by one?" Diego sighs.

"It's like a rosary," I say.

He comes to my bed, sits on the edge, pale and uncertain. Diego looks as if he expects the bed to rock and sway. He has a

syringe and a vial. Then he places a damp towel on my forehead. It
is not creamy and embossed like the towels at the Hotel de la Noche
Roja, where I did not bathe him. There are clutches of flowers in my
throat or I would tell him this. I would make him recant and con-
fess. Diego finds a vein in my wrist where the needle will fit. Most
of my veins have collapsed, sunken in sand with the other rubble at
the bottom of the ocean. Diego is good with his hands, steady, accurate. My lungs taste it, an inflorescence of foxglove, hyacinth.
Perhaps I speak. Perhaps I sleep.

Then it was summer and we were married. Everything
stopped like it did just before the trolley car collision. There was an
incandescent gap like I imagine strangulation must be. I knew precisely what I wanted.

If I could make Diego beautiful, if I could find that capacity
for reinvention, if I could love this ugly man with his appetites
showing, contemptuously flagrant, then I could navigate anything. If I could take Diego, with his voraciousness and greed, I
would prove my strength. Diego, the killer, the butcher, with his
braggadocio infidelities and the women he accumulated like
antiquities or stamps. If I could live with this, I could survive any
circumstance.

Diego's audition requirements were trivial compared to
mine. He was looking for newspaper stories. He was trawling from
habit and for amusement. If I could find a way to avoid being swallowed in the complex gulf of Diego, with his criminal intentions,
with his thief heart and wanton bandit mouth, with his gypsy rum

fat man dances, I could learn to paint. I could shed my plaster cast and drift above the shells of cities. I would be beyond ruin and tarnish. I would see my face in the mirrors of deserted rooms. I would be in a state of grace.

"You have lied most completely about the Hotel de la Noche Roja," Diego says, voice stern, nodding to emphasize his displeasure. Diego, in the guise of a village priest talking to a woman who has strayed. "You insisted. It was your idea absolutely. You weren't even dressed like a woman. I didn't force you. Admit it. And the bracelet. The diamond bracelet. Would I make so bourgeois a statement? No. That never happened. Another falsehood."

In our private darkness, we are all becoming sketches to one another. We are not savages loping through sunken forests, leaving gnawed bones behind when we break camp. Flints and arrowheads. No, we are not barbarians in hotel suites, but a new-world fashion in marriage.

I do not speak. I do not defend myself. I am waiting for more rain. The rain will answer for me, with its azure mouth. Hydrangea. It has all the right answers.

"You are a naughty girl, Frida," Diego says, in his sad mountain village priest's voice. In his starving pueblo voice, his vultures-on-goat-and-mud-ruts voice. The campesino is tragic. I am still silent. "I called you my little school girl, remember? You begged to sit on my lap. We were both shy. I called you little student. I asked what you learned in school that day. I removed your white school uniform blouse. One button at a time. I was gentle. Sometimes I called you daughter."

Is the panther gentle? Is the sea? The rain? The night? Diego had an arsenal of tools for his survival. He pulled rabbits out of hats. He pulled gold coins from sheered air. He threw confetti that dazzled like fireworks. It made you forget the trajectory of your thoughts, accusations, what you suspect, even the evidence you hold in your hands, what you see with your own eyes. Diego had a fabulous bag of tricks. And I will tell you this absolutely. Gentleness was not one of his gifts.

Our marriage day was a paralysis, a stalled pause where we terrorize ourselves. Frida, what a horrible mistake you are making, and with such calculation. I realized that the fall from grace is deliberate. We edge closer to cataclysm. We sense flames, disjointed wind, and sirens. Vegetation is singed and brittle. A band of children with their eyes clawed out pass to our right, their feet bleeding. We move toward them, follow them. We know exactly what we are doing. We long to be burned and then we are.

We stood before the judge. I knew then the anatomy of my desire. I tasted its squalor. I was a liar. I craved adrenaline. I thought in sad red neon and scars. I had divested myself of convention. I was completely exposed. My marriage was a litany of mourning, of clarity at the juncture where I should have said no, should have run. But how can a woman with crushed vertebrae run?

The ceremony was like an autopsy. Then it was over. We were in all the newspapers, forty-two-year-old Diego Rivera and his twenty-two-year-old art school wife. His indigenous wife with Mexican dresses and beads and face the color of baked clay. It was curious how the camera accommodated this. I was disturbingly photogenic. Magazines talked of our Communist politics, which pleased Diego. Newspapers offered our travel itinerary, as if the selected cities might wish to plan celebrations.

"They treat us like cinema stars," Diego observed, stacks of papers from capitals in Europe on the floor, at his feet. "Look at the American coverage." Diego was enthusiastic.

I had passed my audition. I had deliberately fallen from grace. I was his wife legally. I considered dispensing with the Tehauna costumes, unsuitable for American winters. I wanted to broach this subject with Diego, but I suspected they would be permanent. I suspected he would insist.

"Frida. You must be a trademark to be a footnote," Diego reminded me, crumpling a newspaper in his fist the way he might a lone stray bird. I glanced at his hands, imagined him pulling bats from the night air.

I was a wife. A concubine. I should rinse ginger into my hair. I know there is cinnamon and ash in the well. Still amber water. Pond under cathedral bells. Outside were grays, a confusion of asphalt and thunder.

I retrieved the newspaper. I studied a photograph that did not reveal my polio-withered leg, or my splintered bones, how they textured my flesh with ridges and plateaus. They used spoons and miniature hatchets to scrape out my womb. My ruffles and pleats hid this. Fabric defined me. Thin silver earrings, market stall beads. They thought my costume asserted loyalty to my culture, and solidarity with the workers, the masses. They did not recognize the obvious theater that we were.

Diego taught me the value of consistency. I would always be his peasant bride. I was the political statement no one could question. And the glass beads and amulets of Aztec deities were designed to draw the eye, especially the camera eye, away from my flesh, that vessel of ruin, and into the fabric, the regional narrative. I was a history that breathed. I was an image in which Diego and I both conspired. In this, I was a canvas we both painted.

I was deliberate in my manipulation of the ordinary. I was subtle. Who would suspect the cotton drape of my skirt covered wounds? I wore squash blossoms on my neck. There were handembroidered borders below my knees, at my waist, my wrist. And a cigarette. The smoke screen, Diego called it.

"You need bits of business to keep your privacy in front of the camera," Diego told me. "The cigarette as smoke screen. That is good."

Diego employed the language of theater and cinema. We weren't painters. We were a vaudeville team. Films had made painting public and international. Diego said we were like Greta Garbo and John Gilbert. We were Dietrich and von Sternberg.

Didn't their gestures become, inevitably, emblematic? Weren't their eyes a sort of canvas? You could sail on such faces. You could paint on them.

I would let the camera speak for me. I would permit only one dimension. But there would be no dialogue. I would be inaccessible, exotic, and remote. I would be a wall to write on. I would be a public alley where women spit, a man leans against stone while another man kneels at his waist. I would be hieroglyphics for which there is no key.

We had our camera faces and we had our private lives. This distinction later became muted, what was fraudulent, what was authentic. But in the beginning, we had our selves and our contrived public personae. This was the conceptual element in our art. My spine was also conceptual. In actuality, it was held in temporary place by carpentry nails and surgical pins. I was crushed and only the force of my will sustained my body, made it move. No one knew my name was Pierre. I was a portable decoration, like a piñata. I was photogenic. The camera was a tongue and I said lick. There was the juncture of clarity, the stalled gap like a forgotten dried orchid, that paralyzed moment when I did not run.

We were married in August and arrived in San Francisco on the tenth of November. I thought, this will be my final initiation into autumn, the northern and modern. Now I will understand, in a mature way, in this port city raked by wind. I will enter into new covenants with my femaleness. I will shed mistaken boundaries. I will dare.

We were met with ceremony and taken immediately from the city, south, to view redwood trees. I felt a great fatigue, as if I had a hit a wall and was now carrying it. We stood on a bluff, ocean below, dark and winterish, unapologetic. There was nothing tropical about it. It was sharp, distinct, cold, waves broke in lines that could have been drawn by scalpel.

Obligatory photographs. I wasn't warm enough in my rebozo, the ochre of adobe at night. It was a day for surgery. I saw endings in the clipped calligraphy of the waves, in the blunt rocks where we stood, in the way Diego looked not only over my shoulder, but beyond it.

I wished then for a daughter. I would tell her everything about autumn. She would comprehend my fierce struggle. I would show her the junctures where I deliberately fell from grace. I would insist she memorize the coordinates.

I stood below redwood trees, radiant with a desire to articulate seasons, to show my daughter how to know and chart them. This is a woman's navigation, organic, deceptive. You know yourself by harbors and rivers. This is your heirloom, your pocket mirror. The storms and accidents and crimes, the outrages and howls, had accumulated in my stomach and now had mass. Then I felt a spasm like thunder inside me, a miniature birth, the size of a violet's mouth. It was electric, amethyst, and it settled inside my womb.

If I did this skillfully, found the capacity to describe the nuances of autumn, its typography and texture, its elegant silence, my daughter would appreciate me. She would recognize the crossroads I chanced upon, the decisions, the bridges I built by hand, bound with strips of my skin. There are gulfs that cannot be crossed in any known fashion. They require body parts as a rite of passage.

Diego was staring beyond me and the unremarkable coastline festooned with absurdly immense trees. Perhaps he was waiting for a new patron or another photograph to be taken.

I imagined my daughter. The exchange of information between us would necessitate both words and gestures. There are instructions that must be recited, postures to observe and practice. This is the basis of ritual, of the currents that define female realms. Perhaps I would light incense and opium. Opium was possible here, in this port city. Diego had smoked it several times with the governor.

I would sit in an adobe-walled courtyard with my baby, who I named then Flora Violetta. I would smoke opium and sing national anthems and lullabies to her. There would be a wrought-iron gate beyond the garden with its fountains crowded with fallen moths, wings like tapestries and stained glass. Parrots in the palms. Scarlet macaws. No clouds. I would hold Flora Violetta's hand, memorizing the bone structure of her fingers. I would read her palm and know precisely where she would be, the exact location, on each of her birthdays. Lisbon. Peking. A train partway to Prague. I would know the names of her lovers, warn her in advance of indolence and treachery, reveal who she would marry, the names of her children.

I stood on a bluff beneath redwoods and held the hand of my clandestine daughter, Flora. I would come to know her hand, each bone and curve of skin, with such intimacy that I would be able to find her in other lives, when I was blind, when I was disguised, when time was completely different. There is paralysis, an unexpected punctuation, and the ordinary dissolves.

I know how you look when you are severed from the predictable, like someone pulled into a river unexpectedly. Or when a twelve-foot metal railing pierces your pelvis, is wrenched out by a stranger, and you are left on a billiard table to bleed to death. I have seen my face in photographs and I am relentlessly the same, starved and stunned, haunted. My face in silhouette is that of a soiled gutter rat. I shouldn't have dared to tell everyone so much. I convinced myself I was hidden behind vines and gaudy drama. I invented a persona. There was a merging and we became one. I was incautious. I admit this. I felt impervious to flame and metal and this has been my undoing.

We were driving south from San Francisco. When we left the bluff above the dangerous coast, I carried Flora with me. She had just been conceived, she was microscopic, but I could feel her, like a splinter. We were escorted through more ghastly redwoods, into some California pueblo with jewelry stores and bookshops and a moldering Spanish mission. Were there grapes and cactus outside? And leaves singed by too much red wind, scraping the bark to something that was not cinnamon? Were we supposed to pray?

Diego and I exchanged glances. I began laughing. Then Diego, laughing also, collapsed winded into my lap. "Very nice," I said, because my English was better than Diego's. "Very quaint. Thank you. Drive on."

The trees looked raped. I decided it was cheerful. Later, I purchased candles. I would burn them in my solitary nights when I was illuminated by rage. I would explain to Flora the way of women in November, when the peculiar edge is exposed with its faint translucent pulse, with its desire to break. I already knew my nights would be solitary, that Diego would abandon me in an American city of bridges and wind.

"It's an ugly forest," Diego sighed. "It's distorted. Do you like it?"

I shook my head, no. "It's too aggressive," I decided. Diego kissed my hand.

The redwoods were malignant. They possessed dirty secrets. A man they were told to call Uncle had ripped their panties off. There were stains. Mama said it was a lie, her boyfriend would not do such a thing. She tried to show her body to her mother, how her small vagina was outlined with red welts. How her buttocks looked as if a fist had attempted to drill a tunnel through her. You disgust me, the mother said. How dare you take your skirt off in the kitchen? I'll have you locked up with lunatics who think they're saints. Then she slapped her daughter across the face. This will not happen to you, I told Flora with my mind.

"*Basta*," I said. I told Diego I was tired. "It's a sordid forest," I said. "Fuck them."

The trees were intrusive and I wanted to leave. It was a spoiled coast. I saw skeletons on the sides of roads, carcasses, skulls, serrated hands and ears browning in indifferent piles. Diego produced a bottle of tequila. "You must drink," Diego said. "It will calm you."

"You are infinitesimal," I realized. "So afraid to offend the americanos. You fucking coward. Insect. You'd kiss the postman's ass for a commission. Besides, I'll fall asleep. I'll vomit on the curves."

"I've explained your fragile nerves," Diego comforted, placing the tequila in my hand, helping my fingers wrap around the bottle. And that was the end of it.

Cathedral bells. Light rain mixed with wind. Late afternoon, perhaps. Nurse's hair smells of meadow grasses and mottled leaves. Damp. Absence. Erasure. We become sketches to one another. Vignettes. Rubbed-away edges. We lose the dates, the methods. We misplace our children. We are blind from crying. We have tumors in our brains. We hatch embolisms.

"Are you here to take my pulse?" I ask. "I still live."

"You will live forever," Diego proclaims. His voice is strained. The lamp is on. His shirt is soiled, chin stubble, a shadow under his eye like the residue from a street fight.

"What do you want?" I demand.

"Speak with refinement," Diego warns. He is dangling the medicine chest key.

"Demerol," I remember. "Demerol, please."

"I want to know what you dream." Diego lights a cigarette, places it between my fingers. "I want to know if monsters dream."

"I dream the dreams of a serial killer," I say. This is true.

"Tell me." Diego is interested.

"The serial killer dreams of mother. It's summer. Hot. Dry. Mother wears a white cotton dress printed with wisteria and peonies," I begin. I close my eyes to see better.

In California, I vomited on the curving road, winding through cliffs above the Pacific. I slept in the car, my hair foul.

"An americana?" Diego is attentive. He is holding something in his hands.

"Yes. Mother carries a wicker basket of just-picked apples. They are translucent, skin like seasick infants. The serial killer wants to remember this image. He will steal a knife and tattoo the date on a six-year-old."

"That's a lie," Diego says. "Continue."

"Mother is red-wine drunk," I say.

"A dismal vintage? Americanos in the campo?" Diego considers table wines.

"Mother wears a red kimono, stands on Spanish tile, pretending to be a dancer. Someone is pushing her on a battered wooden swing. Her shoe falls off and she is laughing. She is eating pears. She is saying it isn't dinnertime. It is tulip time and pink flamingo time. Mother eats petals and feathers."

"You eat garbage," Diego says. "You like rotting meat."

I close my eyes. I extend my fingers and they twitch. Diego is hiding his fists behind his back. "Which hand?" He is smiling.

"The left," I try.

"I didn't know you could dream," Diego muses. "I thought it too human. You surprise me." He opens his palm. A glass vial. Morphine from the medicine cabinet, which is locked.

"I want Demerol," I tell him.

"You have your Demerol hidden. Crawl to it," Diego says. "Crocodile."

He watches me take the vial. My flesh. The syringe into the glass. Scoop up, the river flows up. No boundaries.

"Have a party," Diego says. He is closing the door. He is gone.

It is now and I am dying.

We were installed in the apartment in San Francisco that had been arranged for us. Diego was painting a mural in the Stock Exchange. Diego the Communist was painting a capitalist shrine. He said it was an act of sabotage. He was subtly poisoning his pigments. He was actually not on scaffolds, but rather the theoretical barricades. He was inciting with his images, his subliminal assertion of a pan-American unity, his vision of the campesino. I was intrinsic to this narrative. That is why he married me.

He ate their caviar-and-champagne lunches and oyster-and-steak dinners. The foods and wines pleasantly surprised him. He shrugged, a man overwhelmed by circumstance and paradox. Poor Diego. He was gone early and home late.

"Don't leave me yet," I said. "Wait a bit. I'm still frightened."

"That is music to my ears," Diego said.

"Please, Diego." I felt my throat constrict.

"Will you beg me on your splintered knees?" Diego seemed interested.

"Yes," I said.

"Don't bother. And don't tell me what to do. I will walk out a door and go to China." Diego was angry. "I don't require permission."

The first night he did not return to the apartment, I became an archaeologist of autumn. I knew the anatomy of fall. I dissected it. Late November. This is when tragedy goes out of remission. Do not answer the doorbell, the telephone in the lobby. What is there to say, anyway? My husband is my enemy? He has left me alone in a foreign city in wind and I am rawer than you know. I am what happens after the rake, what the architecture of bare bark implies. I am sheer wire under lamplight. I am the look that cuts. And don't call me back. Fuck you. Fuck your patrons. Fuck your mother.

It was a full-moon night, a hooked-eye-behind-sea-clouds night. Outside, the gutted stars in their coral burrows. The moon in her multiple identities, hanging like drying clothes on balconies. Or a flank on a meat hook.

Our apartment was graceless, with too many stark empty walls, too many windows, too many views. A bitter lemon light infiltrated from the street. It had the density and oily sheen of neon above a bar. It was a night of stranded moths. I opened a bottle of brandy, put it to my mouth. I didn't need a glass. I suddenly under-stood the perverse region insomniacs feed on.

In this dark you are watching a woman spread eagle on dirt. She is familiar. This is a rape enacted by firelight and lantern. Then she is brought to a holy man. She is blessed and then strangled.

I envisioned women in other apartments, across the boulevard and alleys. They had walked home from work or taken cable cars, stopped in a corner tienda, bought milk and bread and a pint of whiskey. Alcoholics must purchase legitimate items with their intoxicants. They must camouflage their weakness. They fear the opinions of others, though they pretend otherwise.

The women of California are alone. They form a subterranean lattice no one dares speak of. They have buried husbands or been betrayed, used and discarded. Speech becomes a mockery. The mouth is a carved thing, like a statue or an ornament. Or a face in a photograph.

The women of San Francisco share a collective sigh, pour another gin and tonic. We know the abandonments are deliberate, the infidelities trivial. When Diego returned, I would remain in his apartment with my body, but I would shut off my interior machin-ery. I would erase a man as enormous as Diego. I would move around him like a mouse tracing the periphery of rooms. I would make choreography of it. Not even our shadows would collide.

I stood as if my face was soldered to the cold windowpane. I was a moth in reverse, drunk on the draft. The women in other apartments were greenhouse women, blossoming behind glass.

They had the dreams of plants. They inhabited anonymous rooms, minimally furnished, utilitarian, generic. Everything is beige, dirty cream, and brown. It is a decor for women without personal vestiges. Such women have divested themselves of cousins and aunts, the family doctor, the baker who knows your name, the priest who married your parents. Some women prefer absence. They have evolved from a set of circumstances so monumentally painful that they must be shed absolutely. Some women run from their homes with only the clothes on their back. Some women run naked, without shoes, without visas. This is called running for your life.

A blonde across the boulevard swept her kitchen floor. She looked sturdy and bewildered, as if she had abruptly come from the campo. In her posture, I saw roads of weed, stream dark, trickle in shadows. I imagined her speaking the slow sweet English drawl of the South, with its sense of flowers and slow-moving rivers. Mississippi. Magnolia. Moon. Mama.

Perhaps a personal disgrace had brought her to this port city. A passion with a residue. An incaution. Bad luck. Or a not even whispered proclivity that gnawed and made her vulnerable to drift. She forgot names, the rules of multiplication, when Easter was and why it was supposed to be important.

A Chinese grandmother, bent in a baggy old man's sweater, watered herbs on her windowsill. Her daughter and granddaughters visited often. They peeled carrots and what might have been an enormous purple squash. Later, they hung laundry from their balcony. Their laughter was spontaneous. I felt part of their family. I wanted to join in their domestic procedures. I longed to tell them about my own daughter, Flora Violetta.

One A.M. Two A.M. No Diego. I stood at the window all night. I understood why women wear veils, how they come to crave the protecting mesh. It filters out the sudden, the intrusive, the brutal remarks and their cumulative effect. A woman could become immune to insult and entreaty. She could create unusual forms of disguise. She could convince herself that it was a necessity of survival and a mark of integrity.

The women of November came from an identical conceptual desert. I had seen this California underbelly from railroads and highways. The stucco tenements. The field-side shack and trailer park. Rib-high corn in vacant lots. Sand blowing in from the east. Low gritty horizon. Squalid orange trees. The November women sit in cubicles the color of dried urine, knitting, darning, embroidering by stray street light. They must keep their fingers moving so they don't gouge out their eyes.

When you do not sleep, you develop theories of the unconscious. All women with unfaithful husbands know this. And women who are pregnant, particularly women who carry concealed babies. And women who have recently been widowed or miscarried. Women with menopause and hot flashes, who wake up shivering, with bedsheets soaked. Women with actual names, dates, and locations for their sins. Women who smoke in bed, counting out their nights in matches and miniscule flames. Women who sleep with dolls. Women who sleep with photographs and trinkets in their hands, under the pillow. Women who pretend they have slit their wrist with razors and bandage themelves. Women who drink too much brandy and sleep with the radio playing. Women who wake up crying.

When you are insomniac, you sense the forests of longing within. They are like autumn oceans, where apple orchards float. Our grandmothers are there, necks scented with tea rose, mouths sherry. They wear glass bracelets in tarnished brass settings. They are saying they carried these pieces of costume jewelry across mountain ranges wrapped in rags taped to their bodies. They carried these objects in their private crevices. These anecdotes are recited through generations. What the grandmothers offer is not truth, but rather an approximation. As the story is repeated, there are mutations, in the one who speaks, and in the one who listens. In this way, all we ever exchange are forms of fiction.

We dangle between vignettes. We do ask why they carried worthless fragments across a continent, the glass and copper brooch they couldn't barter for a loaf of black bread or half a chicken. We pretend these acts of stupidity are the enactment of moral and aesthetic principles.

This is why we sleep. We dream to forget them and their stilted improvisations. Still, we are giving our children the names of people we hated. This is the rattle in autumn thunder. This is why we are deaf. This is the reason for lung problems, consumption, pneumonia.

I was growing a baby named Flora. Someday we would smoke opium together in the gardens of the Casa Azul. We would read

Rimbaud and Freud and Russian novels in French. I would teach Flora to identify herbs and flowers.

Just before sunrise I left my perch at the window. I painted by candlelight, naked, on the kitchen floor, my paints in teacups and saucers on top of newspapers that might have contained my photograph. I shivered but I was not cold. Then I painted by dawn light.

Diego returned the next night, hungry, energetic, clapping his hands, making the gestures of the theater in the small entranceway. He was humming, running water for a shower, switching on the radio. Opera. He suggested dinner, Italian, of course, the city was only possible for pasta and fish. Then a party, maybe two.

"You've been painting," an ebullient Diego observed. "It's ugly. Childish. Completely inept. You are an embarrassment."

So it would continue. The days and nights redolent with junctures, gouged, like the abscesses on my back. Then Diego would return, offer an entertainment and I would agree, dress, apply face paints, elaborate layers of ribbon and flowers in my hair. I didn't have clothing. I had costumes. I didn't have a marriage. I had a form of traveling theater. I let circumstance define me.

It was the era of cinema. Diego often spoke of the power of film and image. One must consider the implications of lighting and wardrobe. Most important, one had to be recognizable, like a nun or a peasant or a policeman. Image was an opiate the masses could comprehend. Think of Garbo with her cheekbones and harbor eyes. And Marlene with her whore's legs and man's tuxedo.

"We are all actors now," Diego declared, spraying imported perfume on his neck. "Get dressed."

I kept my quadrant of jungle in a steamer trunk. It was theater. It was vaudeville. Diego and I were a team for the stage.

I found beads and a bracelet composed of miniature machetes, knives, and hearts. This was how I said I hate you. I dressed for dinner. I brushed my hair, braided it with pink ribbons and pink silk flowers. Pink for atrocity, for scars and burns and girl babies. Diego was conducting a radio symphony using a brush as a baton.

Diego was uncontainable. He wore his appetites like a leper his sores. He was a leper in reverse. No ochre rags and foul odor, no loss of body parts. Instead, Diego accumulated women and bloat, commissions and cities. He was expanding.

"More paint," Diego yelled above the music. "On your face, idiot."

I was a creature of kohl and rouge. Compromise made me glow. I was lit by my deceptions and crimes. I clarified the marrow of fall and purified it. It tasted like wounded sherry. I could drink it, dab it in my cuts, use it for bath oil. I was becoming immune to contagion. I deciphered whispers on the barbed wire periphery. I knew what pulsed barely coalesced in the static.

Somewhere, a woman burns her furniture to stay warm. She paints by candlelight, squatting naked on newspapers like a dog being trained. She knows candles are not a kitchen gift. They are surgical instruments for women who dare the current, who turn toward the dark. Women who risk the abrasion of wind. When the wax melts, they can use their flesh for light, their thigh, their left fourth finger, the ring one. That's the finger I plan to burn off first.

Diego and I were joined by subterfuge. We were wrapped in damaged light, in what had become of night, in its sordid remnants. I wore the rags of evening, plum like a bruise, a wound, a wine stain across linen.

I looked in the mirror, admiring my singularity. My image. The embodiment of a Diego Rivera fantasy. My eyes were twin wells. Diego insisted I do nothing to disguise the dark hairs across my top lip. He called it an ambiguity. I took a sip of brandy. My face watched me drink. I noticed my eyebrows grew together like a hideous black bridge, as if my thoughts wanted to march out and cross over, into another skull.

Then it was Diego's season of red-haired women. They had heads like American pennies. They had tresses like iodine. They were tint-ed orange and auburn and russet. They were wearing autumn on their heads. Their earrings rattled. Americanas. They would wear perfume scraped from the dead if it brought them closer to celebrity.

Diego came and went. There were the scaffolds at the Pacific Stock Exchange Luncheon Club where lobster and oysters and brandy were served to the men who had built the railroads. Diego rarely missed this. Then the mural at the California School of Fine Arts. And the parties, of course, where Diego hunted for patrons. It was sport for him. Scenting and identifying them. Then the tracking and wooing, the coy dance, the fake surprise.

I was his miniature jungle bird, decorated with turquoise and obsidian, flaws hidden. They could see us across a room. We were stylized, like an intricate tango with an entire psychology and politics. Diego wore his wide-brimmed hat. He twirled his silver-plated pistol. I made him seem, simultaneously, larger and more accessible. I sparkled, like cuff links that walk, drink too much, and invent vulgar anecdotes. I was a dog on a glittering leash or a monkey curled around his neck. Some already suspected I smoked opium. Who would take my painting seriously? It was early December and the red-haired women were painting their nails gold.

The bay wind was a form of sculpture. It changed my ideas and dimensions, my scale. It blew in, transforming. It could be savage. It could seduce. I was painting with regularity, my hand more consistent, fearless.

Diego found a copper-head with a father who owned every sawmill in a province called Oregon. She had ulcers and kept drinking rum and gin. She coughed blood and pretended it didn't happen. The first night Diego took her to bed, she hemorrhaged and flushed it away, sprayed perfume on her neck and walked with satin high-heeled sandals trimmed with fur back to their bed. She tapped her champagne glass with a gold-tipped finger, indicating a desire for more.

"What élan." Diego was appreciative. "So distinctively American."

"When I engage in such behavior, you say I'm demented." I paused, examined my paintbrush, and evaluated the dusk, the light and shadow. A sense of the harbor rising.

"That is because you are a whore," Diego said. "You are sub-human. She is magnificent."

Often I had bouts of pain. I felt my eyes would fall out from the pressure. I gagged on water. At such times, I could drink nothing. That's when opium became important. When I was well, I tried to heal my demolished spine with whiskey. The amulets I needed were liquid and amber. When I could get out of bed I painted, naked, on newspapers, like a bad dog, a leaking dog, half asleep in its stink.

From our apartment at sunset, the city was subtle, rose and gold, open and subdued, racked with a slow fever of cloud. The hills across the bay were pastel. Perhaps I could be reformed, made whole in salt waters. I could be baptized like adults in the American South who hallucinate Jesus Christ in jail cells or in taverns. They are immediately forgiven, restored, and called reborn. I would enter the water alone. I might be accepted by the current, born under the orange bridge, and wake on a beach in China. I would ask for a Chinese name that contained a quality of the soul like patience or faith or celebration.

At night, lights below Russian Hill looked like atoms of neon or the pulse of drugs in a vein. They looked like love. I had found the illuminated perimeter, the wires with their gold electric. Then I painted. Diego had a new woman, of course. She had hair like a glazed maple.

"Spare me the litany of the family riches," I said.

"Don't you want me to be happy?" Diego looked surprised. He was holding his silver-plated pistol, contemplating it with affection.

"You are becoming tedious," I said. I did not have to talk to Diego. I could paint. I could smoke opium. I could drink. I could watch the harbor, ships rushing beneath the orange bridge to be anchored before dawn. I could envision their cargoes and where they had been.

"I bore you?" Diego turned from the mirror.

"Yes." Cargoes of northern fish, perhaps, pelts for coats. Antique chairs and armoires inlaid with mother-of-pearl.

"You hurt me, Chiquita. You give me pain. Let me make love to you now." Diego motioned me to him. "I will return the favor."

I was hospitalized twice for infection of my abscesses. There were additional plaster casts. Then the dizziness and fever passed. I returned to the apartment on top of Russian Hill.

When I was well, I went into the city alone. Diego was gone. I rode cable cars. I took a taxicab across the Golden Gate Bridge. I walked slowly up and down hills. Sometimes I took my daughter, Flora, with me. I was not bound by the rules of ordinary motherhood. When it was convenient, I left Flora alone, back in the apartment. I turned the radio on, so she wouldn't be lonely. She was portable. I could take her out of my womb. I could return her by spreading my legs wide, and using a brush or spoon, push her back into the mossy nest in my uterus. She was not yet formed, so she could not speak. She had other places inside me where she lived. She had found a crevice in my spine where nerves wrapped her, like kelp in a sea. The boundaries were fluid. Just like my marriage and the rules that govern canvas. There were none.

I could still walk then, up and down narrow streets smelling of coffee, baking bread, and slow sunlight across sedate waves. There were intricacies in the wind, some conjunction of spices and bits of tin or sail perhaps.

In a display case window, pearl necklaces and carved ivory masks. My skin was a sequence of leaves at the bottom of a teacup waiting to be sifted. I lived in a house of mirrors. There were more than three dimensions. Hieroglyphics were etched just beneath the flesh of my ribcage and back. You would need special instruments to find them. It would take centuries to translate. I was eroding. From certain angles I did not have scars. Night breezes had washed them off, neon lights and riding fast in cars.

The brown hills across the bay reminded me of the flesh of abandoned women, exiled, discarded, of no use to anyone. They had no eggs, had borne no sons. Some man had taken a new concubine and sent them away. Dismissed with contempt. Be as you were, empty, starving by a riverbank. Return to reeds. Maybe the earth will love you. He pointed his finger in the direction of the wilderness and she went.

Silence was a harbor also, with a shape and levels, it defined and contained, elongated and deepened. There were birds as I wound down cobblestone and dirt alleys to Chinatown. I considered visiting missions, the famous one in San Juan Capistrano, near the border with Mexico, where the birds continually return, obsessive swallows. They are drawn back yearly to the walled adobe church where they hear the bells but do not understand them. Bits of prayer rise from cactus and dust, hedges of sallow parched oleander. The scratching of branches and swarm of swallows. Perhaps sound is a kind of alphabet one can comprehend simply by the act of receiving air and listening to rustling leaves the color of burned saints. We do not live in homes, I thought, not in villas or apartments perched on hills above harbors, not in shacks on beaches or cul-de-sac river backwaters. We live in aviaries.

I walked fast, hearing the off-rhythm my shoes made on the sidewalk, step and drag, step and drag, left for stepping, right for dragging. I still had two legs then. I had ten toes. They thought they could fix me. I heard my shoes on the pavement, a sequence I was trying to hammer into the ground, a series of signals that burrowed under and echoed somewhere else, like gongs. Perhaps I was talking to myself in the future or in a port where I had not yet been. I was welcoming the self that had not yet come. Much of life is preparation for what does not happen. Then we are naked and startled by the obvious.

Consider Joan of Arc, not a saint but a displaced woman. An ordinary woman who chanced to be in an accident, a collision. This caused her to appear as an aberration in her mistaken circumstance. Her clothing was wrong. When such women are noticed, attention is usually unfortunate. Threats. Interrogation. They have acres of answers but they are not allowed to speak. Then their tongues are removed. They are skinned while conscious and weeks pass before they die. A temporary roof of red and yellow silk scarves once covered the Coliseum in Rome. The sky was erased. Blood was remote under the mist of silk.

In Chinatown, ducks and chickens hung in shop windows. They looked lacquered and molten, as if they had been tortured. Should you eat them or wear them as beads? I thought of the ports of antiquity, with wharves for trading foods and selling slaves and women. That is what docks are for, in every century. Barter and flesh and contraband.

Chinatown was a region for bandits and renegades. I liked this. I thought, yes, you have come home. This is where you belong, Frida. You are safe. I stood in gutters and alleys where markets were decorated with defiled fowl red as condensed dragons. We live in aviaries near ports where wares are exhibited and sold and some of the cargo is alive. It is taken to brothels and prisons. It is taken into restraints and hospitals and then you are forced to take medicines that tranquilize. That is what doctors do to women who complain about their condition. They are sedated. Say you adore your cast, with your rat-infested concept of a body encased within. Say their treatments are sublime. Of course your bones are healing. Of course they don't feel gritty like sand pushing through the scarred flesh. Say you are improving steadily. Your wounds are not festering rank in their own private fall. Pretend they do not exist. If you dare to wonder out loud, they will put you to sleep for the day or ten days or ten years. Perhaps, like a dog leaking from eyes and mouth, they will put you to sleep forever. This is often termed compassion. But this will not happen to me. I am twenty-two and the wife of Diego Rivera. I will buy my opium and go directly home. Believe me, I won't bother you again.

Cristina, angel of bells and rain and morphine. Calm now or perhaps exhausted. Bitch husk.

"Did he send you?" I ask.

"He's sleeping." She sits on a straw chair near the shutters, which are opened.

"Is he having nightmares?" I laugh. I gesture for a cigarette. I point to my wrist where I put the Demerol in. Nurse has come already. Perhaps Cristina doesn't know.

"You are the nightmare," Cristina lets me know. "And you are a bad girl, Frida."

"It's my specialty," I admit. "Unrepentant heresy."

Out the window, chartreuse leaves. The day is without shadow. Noon is a port of inflamed green. I point to the vein on my wrist.

"Not yet." Cristina, patient or broken and wanting something. "It's still the same day."

"Is this a death vigil?" I am startled awake, try to sit up. I am paralyzed.

"You are extremely sick. Do you comprehend that? Your situation?" Cristina looks past the window, to a shelf holding lacquered bowls and hair combs, a carved stone frog from Chile.

"So I am dying?" I am surprised. "Without the little bells from Oaxaca?"

Cristina the silent. Composed. Infinitely tolerant. She will give me Demerol. I will tell her where it is hidden.

"Is it the same day?" I ask. So many numbers. Equations. Orbits. Enamel and bone, a branch, a cathedral, a ruby ring.

"It's the same day, but afternoon now," Cristina says. She gestures toward the window. "See the sun between storm clouds?"

"How old am I?" I am confused. I am twenty-two.

"Forty-six. You will be forty-seven soon. On your birthday," Cristina explains.

"Then I won't have time to finish." I feel astonishment and grief.

"That is the nature of things," Cristina, matron of the rainy green afternoon, agrees. She does not ask me what I will not finish.

"What will I do?" I am desperate. My voice does not betray this, remains distant, languid.

"Become more selective," Cristina offers. "Concentrate on the headlines. You've never had a problem doing that."

Then she is gathering objects. A pen from her apron pocket. A sheath of papers appear. "Do you want me to write anything? A letter, perhaps? A message?" Cristina regards me. She is hopeful, vigilant, persistent.

"Fuck you. I'll deliver it myself," I scream.

So, it is the same day. It is a death vigil. A death vigil for Frida. I spit at my sister. I throw an ashtray. I break a lamp. I get Demerol anyway.

Chinatown. And I won't be able to finish. How I wandered, limping streets and alleys arranged by product. Fish and cakes, teak boxes, birds in cages, gold rings. Alley of oysters and crab. A market of aberrant fruits and my impulse is to smell and touch each one. My hands and eyes say yes. What ravishment in this lacquered purple, this flagrant yellow. Hold this orb, this sphere that looks painted, cool and smooth as a stone the sea has intimately polished. Of course there are forms of knowledge that can only be imparted through the fingertips. Certain complexities are tactile, they must be traced with pieces of the body. Some truths involve rituals of flesh. That is why we must place our daughters on our laps while we recite the vignettes we call the story of our lives.

Shops of dusty ovals I recognize as roots. They had dug in. They knew. Then I was entering the avenue of birds. I am Diego's twisted bird. I agreed to this. Mute parrot. An adornment. A few seeds and I amuse. If the harvest disappoints, I could be put on a spit or boiled. And the birds are behind me, enraged in their cages, staining the air at my back. Then alleys with grotesque poultry stuck on hooks, shrunken and suspended. They are like women in plaster casts that are perpetually drying.

Every street in Chinatown was a point of entry. I was startled by the fish markets. Afternoon stalled as I entered, as if it were me, Frida, rather than the dead fish, that could not get enough air into her lungs. I felt becalmed. Fish on beds of ice, all their eyes wide open. A vague odor that might have been an attribute of sunlight and fog.

The fish were a mysterious gray like the essence of late afternoon waters in November. Their mouths were uniformly open, as if in a collective chant. The fish eyes were bulging and they were all facing the same direction. They were staring at the point on the compass where Buddha was. I should remember the angle, find the coordinates, make calculations, purchase a map and globe. Then I would know where to plant crops to avoid flood and drought.

On an alley sweet with almond cookies and honey cakes, I decided to buy Diego a gift. I stood in an enormous mart crowded with tea sets and dishes with entire sagas painted along the rims and borders where you might place your lips. Diego would place his lips anywhere.

On shelves were things that looked like fetuses in jars. Then what might have been unusual sticks. Were they used for cooking, acts of magic, or sex? Were they for divining or did you push them into the crevices of someone you briefly love? I was suddenly glad I had left Flora back in the apartment. I had placed her in my ring box so I wouldn't drop or spill her.

At the bottom of a steep hill, I stood in a roofless arcade stacked with representations of the Buddha. Perhaps Diego would like him. Buddha, with his fat belly and satisfied face looking as if he just solved the ultimate equation and decided to tell no one, to burn his notebooks, to watch them float like parched lilies, to be taken by the current under the Golden Gate Bridge.

Aisles of Buddhas, carved wood and stone, painted and glazed. Now he is serious. Now he is decadent, leaning back after drinking too much sake, perhaps. Here he is, bloated, holding what might be a ledger. I thought of Diego, with his private leather book of commissions, divided into categories of possible, probable, and certain. And how would I know when I found the right Buddha?

I touched carved teak and cherrywood. I ran my fingers over marble and granite, bronze, jade. Nothing stung or burned. There was no caress, no sense of resolution. The Buddha was fattened with arrogance, like a pedophile. And then with a devious alegría, he looked like Diego. He, too, had the expression of one who expects to live for millennia.

I held a Buddha constructed from a material that mimicked gold, a metal that cut my finger. Kiss this Buddha and your mouth will fill with blood. I didn't need an idol for that. I had Diego. After Diego's kiss, you needed more than a tissue or bandage. You needed a tourniquet.

In a shop for hairdressing, where young Asian women smiled their many lies that do not require translation, I had my nails polished. I chose a brutal red called Dragon Lady. Near me, an altar of sand held peacock feathers and stale incense with names of spices and flowers and psychological states like purity, devotion, and grace.

I had two legs then. Ten fingers. Ten toes. I walked in sun, wind, mist, rain, absorbing the climates of Chinatown. I was painted by cloud. I was a canvas, a landscape. At 4 P.M., at the start of dusk, the little boy who led me to the opium seller would appear. I would follow him through alleys, to a steep wooden stairway, around a sharp turn, into a tunnel. The floor would be sand. Rough wood for benches. Candlelight. A stooped man without teeth, hands fluid, graceful, weighing pieces resembling bark into a scale his grandfather might have used. Rolling the opium into newspaper. Behind fabric was a door. I would sit on a blanket in the back room with Chinese and American men and the occasional women, smoking pipes lit by children with quick fingers. Then I was led out, walking quickly with my bag of opium. I bought cookies, bunches of carrots. I looked like any shopper with fish in paper, vegetables for dinner. I was swimming above the sandy floor of an ocean.

After the opium sellers on the Avenue of Sublime Suffering, a fork in the dirt led to the Avenue of Infinite Enlightenment. More Buddhas. I held them in my dragon-painted nails, my rainforest-leaf nails, where I was predator, hungry under festering jade vines. At that moment, I realized there are no simple lines between acts of fraudulence and enchantment.

It's a continuum, with jogs in alleys where we consider tea sets and statues, opiates and breads, an accidental token of a passing decision that changes our lives. At the end of the last alley narrow as an oxcart, saints sprout flowers from their stigmata, orchards rise from the punctures in their nailed palms, orange and peach trees. You could walk through valleys of the beheaded and assemble flower arrangements that would remain fragrant for centuries. Someday, I would paint my wounds to resemble livid rivers with fish in them. Out of my hollowed palms would come thunder. I would show myself as a doe with a Frida face. A startled doe, with sixty-seven arrows and nails from my casts bursting with chrysanthemums.

I watched her approach brazenly, examining my body as she turned from the Avenue of Sublime Suffering. She was carrying a bag similar to mine. She climbed the hill where I stood near the mart of impossible and garish teacups and Buddhas, in their innumerable paradoxes and varieties. I was an idea forming as she walked. I became more substantial, as she defined me, separated me from shadow.

Who remembers what was said? We are incarcerated in camouflaged aviaries, in confetti of competing alphabets, rasp of chickens, gossip of women washing clothing on the banks of summer rivers. It is difficult enough to breathe in and out, remain vertical, and remember one's temporary address.

She had the art school look about her, the universal uniform of abstract devotion, shabby and romantic. Dusty corduroy, a too large cardigan sweater that was listless and shapeless around her shoulders and chest, as if it had given up. Her hair was too long and untethered. She regarded the wind as if she could decipher something profoundly significant in it. She was trying to make herself more attractive to the wind. More vertical and willing. She wore a long red silk scarf popular that year in France. It was a statement of purpose, signifying her interest in mating. She was asserting her availability and how expensive she was.

She gave the impression of being a person who paints or sculpts or works with gold or silver, perhaps. Alloys. Fabrications. Little-girl hands, like mine. No rings. A faint metallic trace emanated from her skin and deliberately ragged clothing, not alcohol or formaldehyde, but something gritty and familiar. A chemical preservative or disinfectant.

Perhaps she spoke first, said, "You look lost." She was Chinese. I could see her eyes behind her sunglasses. Her accent.

"I am completely lost," I might have replied. "First I lost my body. My children. Then I lost my husband, though he was never quite mine. I'm an unofficial widow. And now I've lost my mind."

"What are you looking for?" She placed her hand on her hip, evaluated my face, the texture of my skin, the planes of my cheekbones. Her lips were lined with what fell from tropical island sunset skies in a sequence of scented reds. Her mouth was a permanent August. You could lie down in the lips of such a mouth and summer would stall. You could become a woman of golds and bronzes and forget to go home.

"I am looking for opium," I replied, testing her reaction.

"Avenue of Sublime Suffering. Halfway, stairs down, tunnel to the back room. But you've already been there. I smell it." She stared into me. "You should wear sunglasses."

We were walking idly up a hill on a street of pastries. Avenue of Divine Cream. The air was honey and coconut. She had been in San Francisco five years. She had been born in Shanghai. She was a photographer. I did not tell her I was a painter. I did not tell her that my father had been a photographer. That was the smell I recognized. The acid from the developing solution drifting from her hair and pores, from her red silk scarf. I did not mention my husband, Diego Rivera.

Her Chinese name was unpronounceable, so she called herself Jane. She wanted to take my photograph. I was unique, remarkable. She would make tea. We were winding toward her studio. A man in a beige raincoat, carrying an umbrella under his arm, passed, stared at us. It occurred to me that I could walk down any of the network of branching alleys off the narrow streets with their halibut, and crab and almond, with their back rooms and warehouses of contraband, and a whole other life would begin.

Jane had her own studio. Was she offering me protection, already, without yet viewing my back? Was she outlining her territory? Her father had purchased this building for her. That was after her photographs were displayed in Florence and Berlin. He was a Chinese doctor of the ancient method called acupuncture. "He stops pain with his needles," Jane explained.

"I find such a practice of inestimable value," I replied, following her into the kitchen region of her studio. She had an extensive selection of teas, orange blossom, raspberry, jasmine, and oriental hibiscus.

I imagined myself in a kitchen lined with glistening white shelves and philodendrons. I would keep teas for potency, serenity, and sleep in diminutive glass jars and vials, each labeled in calligraphy with their lyrical names and purported attributes. I would spend afternoons selecting and mixing, brewing and pouring. No one would suspect I was malingering.

"Do you have a job?" Jane asked, playing. Tea bearing the name of an Asian river steaming in a pot. She wanted to be lied to.

"I am a magician's assistant," I tell Jane. Jane. How American. It sounds like a small wad of plastic in my mouth. It's a feeling so abrasive, I begin to like it. "Jane," I say, repeating her artificial name, savoring the sound. "I hold the hand of the woman my partner saws in half. I hold his cloak. I spin the wheel when he throws knives at the revolving woman. Sometimes I am the revolving woman."

"Is this ongoing? Or is it seasonal?" Jane wants to know. She is smiling. She wants me to slap her face. Later, she will want to lick the abscesses on my back. When I am encased in a plaster cast, she will want to straddle me, rub against plaster while I describe what scurries inside my latest corset, roaches, spiders, and miniature dogs.

Jane expects tragedy to ring her doorbell. In between, she smokes opium, takes photographs, and shops.

"It's perpetual. It's the carnival life." I believed that was true. I sighed. "We are international." I clarified.

Jane's loft was on a high floor of an otherwise abandoned warehouse. One entire wall was window. I could sense, without looking, that the light was northern. Jane prepared me for the camera. We lit the opium pipe for one another. I admired the craftsmanship, the carved ivory inlaid with gold. A sleepy Jane agreed. "It is the finest thing I ever stole." She said.

Jane wanted to photograph me in various costumes. With her gold nails, she indicated an alcove where dresses and cloaks hung. A nun's habit and an evening gown. A wedding dress. Feather boas. Strands of paste pearls. A school uniform. Mantillas and lingerie.

"Take off your clothes, OK?" Jane with camera. Professional. Protected. A seduction she can only win. "What are you drinking?"

"Brandy," I said, my rebozo slipping to the dirty loft floor. Then the rest. She led me by the hand to where I should stand or bend or curl. She lit my cigarettes.

Jane took photographs of me naked standing in front of the huge bank of ceiling-to-floor windows with the harbor at my back. My breasts seemed to merge with the domes of buildings on the other side of the glass. I had come to a portal. Jane wanted me to steal her camera. She had toy ideas. Doll intrigues. Did my thoughts show in these photographs, in shadows and patches of sudden fierce light?

"Your scars are fantastic. You're a quilt. Your skin is mottled like marble. And your spine. Ridged. You should be sculpted." Jane talked fast, the camera between us. "Were you born like this?

Defective? Is that why you live in a circus?" Jane. Snap, snap. Voice rapid, breathy. Flash. Snap. "Were you violated? Was it a ritual? An accident with machines?" Jane removed her sunglasses. Soon, she would put the camera down. No more props. No more costumes.

I did not speak about my back, with its war zone of barbed wire perimeter and ditches. In the photographs it would look as if spires were growing from my spine. I would be a landmass where everything was inert and I would be the quietest of all. I would be the core, glass smooth, where ships come to anchor. I would be the Sunday cove. The rows of houses on the hills behind me would be ridges of scale and I would be a dragon lady. I would know exactly what to do. I would offer my face to the winds in the uncountable harbors. I would open my mouth and fire would come out.

"I'll love you like a Dragon Lady would," I said. I motioned her to join me, naked on the wooden floor. I didn't know where the bed was. I didn't care.

"Will it hurt?" Jane lay next to me. Lip trembling. Hair of French perfume and opium.

"Definitely. Are you frightened?" I finished the opium in the pipe. I let my cigarette burn out.

"I'm afraid," Jane said, her eyes half closed. I leaned down, over her. I bit her lip until it bled in a line down her chin. She slowly touched her mouth, stared at the blood on her fingertips, clenched her hands into fists and moaned.

Jane had painted nails. A gold called Fire Woman. In nail salons, women are the keepers of the pinks and reds, the instructions for sculpted extensions and silk wraps. This is a female calligraphy they don't teach in art school.

I watched Jane's gold-painted nails trace my nipples. Lick and pinch. Fire Woman. Torches at the fingertips. This is how you create a moment of flame. You must engrave it into your flesh. This is how you become a lighthouse, the method by which sailors calculate where they are and how to return.

"More intensity," I suggested. Jane had not yet touched my back. Now she traced my breast with her fingernails.

A woman in December must be naked with strangers. Outside was a silky unraveling. I could see the city behind Jane's shoulder. I wanted to lose my mind, here, with molting streets and Chinese alleys with shrimp and herbs for passion, roots for healing bone, Buddhas and tea sets and bamboo mats from Siam and Ceylon.

I threaded my fingers through Jane's black hair. It was long and had the texture of certain woven fishing nets. I considered the possibility that one could have a passion, not for a man or a woman, but for a place and a season. The people were mere catalysts, sketches, cutouts. San Francisco in December. Such love requires a fresh identity. A shedding, forgery, stolen papers.

To love autumn as it wants to be loved, to meet it with equal intensity, would kill you. It would break you like a derailed trolley car. An explosion and gold dust falling into your wounds, a warm rain becoming specific. I watched her gold fingers skim my belly. She would lick each stitch and count them with her tongue. She would trace the gutters in my legs with her mouth. Maybe I moaned.

Later, at the window of the loft, Jane wore a wedding veil while she photographed my back. She leaned me against the enormous window. Jane kneeling, tracing my ridged spine with her fingertips. To look at my disfiguration was not enough. Jane realized she must absorb it with her mouth. She wanted my accidental tattoos to live inside her. She was having an adventure. She stole her ideas. She sucked them out. Jane thought art and the black market were identical.

It was a shadowed afternoon. December wanted to knock my teeth out. It wanted to watch me bleed. It wanted me to smoke opium in neglected back rooms where men have sex with children while gambling on cards and the races of horses, roosters, and dogs. Outside were church bells and the sounds ships make, foghorns, seabirds, taxis, and babies.

I am a Dragon Lady now. We have multiple lives and inhabit them simultaneously. We cannot count the identities we enter and shed, apartments and villas rented and abandoned, whole houses with clothing left on hangers in closets. A pile of piñon and red juniper, cut but not burned. The plans for the veranda patio, the garden waterfall, outlines with ink and numbers left rolled up on thin sheets of architectural paper, everything to scale, somewhere. Such pages remain as surely as ports on maps. These are the passages of water women, the records of where we docked, spent an afternoon or a decade.

Now sunset, plum, aster, violet. It was the dark of a dog bark in an alley where the bus went, onto a highway aimed for the capital and no one turned to wave. I was on the bus that day. I was also in the depot, watching it drive away.

"Will I see you again?" Jane asked. Tremulous. Lips bruised. Bourgeois hypocrite.

"You didn't even see me now," I said.

Jane ran down the stairs, caught my shoulder, made me stop in the street. "You must come here again," she whispered. "Promise."

"No," I said.

Chinatown wasn't quite dark. The neon was insistent, gouging itself into the night. A man with a newspaper under his arm passed without glancing at me, pretending he wasn't prowling.

A woman with red lips like a blister slowly appraised me, stared into my eyes, then abruptly turned away. I could enter any branching alley off the hill boulevards and a whole other existence would begin. I could take a new name, marry a banker, a lawyer, a fisherman. I could study mathematics or philosophy at the university, take sailing lessons, play flamenco guitar.

It was dinnertime and banners were strung across the gaudy crowded streets. I could read them. Banner script repeating phrases from cracked open bellies of fortune cookies. Beauty. Prosperity. Health. Peace. No more casts. No more hospital months. Surgeries. Your plundered eggs will be returned. You are promised dreamless nights, obedient children, and decades of good rice harvest. There is a bridge across a river people must cross. You sit under a bamboo umbrella taxing them, and their sons, and their oxen. You even tax their dogs.

It was a chilly night and Chinatown had just woken up.

Afternoon was merely a prologue. Now the streets were becoming vivid, delirious. Everyone was hungry. A wood-plank store displayed swans constructed entirely from pearls. There were pearl goats and temples carved from ivory. I was still searching for a gift for Diego. A handheld deity, perhaps, or a Buddha to wear around his neck. A silver ornament to match and accentuate his travesty of a pistol.

I was becoming confused by the intricacies of cloisonné, the peonies and carp on vases, serving dishes, and the sheaths of daggers. The legends of owls and snails, frogs, bells, cranes.

I entered a shop displaying herbs resembling dried reptiles. Shelves of tentacled whitish forms looked cramped and alive and clearly planning another ocean crossing. Should a woman come at night and release them? The shop owner explained what the herbs would do. Death. Divorce. Abortion. A limb amputation or restoration. The removal of scars. Stuttering, limping, deafness, stupidity. The erasure of cravings, headaches, recurrent nightmares. A move to another city or country, riches by mail or private messenger. Solace, public absolution, justice, and long life. Perhaps the healing of corns, ulcers, a new mother-in-law and six perfect sons. What was it I wanted?

Diego was savage, face contorted, sweat covering his khaki brother-of-the-masses painting shirt. I thought of the phrase soldier of fortune. Diego was an art mercenary. He wore the colors of war. Then he slapped me across the face.

"You've been fucking. I can tell," Diego yelled. The noise was of no concern. Neighbors had already told the Pacific Stock Exchange and Luncheon Club that they wanted us to move. "And I'm tired," Diego sighed. He stared at a chair near the window with longing. "I've worked all day, my feet hurt. And now I have to decontaminate you."

Diego dragged me by my hair. My day had also been long. The opium. The hills. The other hair pulling. The colossus of Buddhas and tea sets. All that cloisonné. I screamed because my scalp was raw. Diego yanked out a handful of hair. It was an ebony nest in his hand. I needed to open my ring box and see how Flora Violetta was. Perhaps she was hungry or crying. Maybe she was stuck in a metal coil.

He motioned me onto my knees, hands on the edge of the bathtub, in the position for prayer. He turned the hot water on, pushed me forward with his foot, a sharp kick. He was going to scald and then drown me. Soap stung my eyes. He was shampooing my hair, once, twice. I was shivering, kneeling on tile. Diego was slowly running a comb through my scalp, making indentations, temporary roads. Did he think we were going somewhere?

"What are you doing?" I asked.

"Looking for lice. Sailors are filthy with body insects. And syphilis. It burns out their brains like brushfires. You know that. Now stand in the tub." He scrubbed me hard with a wire brush.

Hot water pouring over my head, running down my face, my back.

He took me by the hand, led me to the bed. He fluffed the pillows. I leaned back, felt the silk of the sheets. Outside, the enormous sprawl of harbor with its two lit bridges. The harbor, obsidian, with its prison on an island in the center. That's where Diego and I should live.

"Spread your legs," Diego ordered. "Arch your grotesque spine."

It must have been between casts. I was able to do this. Diego sat near me. He was holding a comb and tweezers. He poured tequila into the soap dish.

"Observe," Diego was stern. Then he made trails with a comb through my pubic hair. He made a lattice with his fingers, a sort of map. He held the comb up to me. A gray lint, perhaps? Diego extracted strands from the comb with a tweezers. They were moving. Then he jabbed the tweezers into the tequila. "It's amazing. Look. Lice have tiny pinchers. Alcohol kills them."

Then he turned me on my belly. He shoved and my back was exposed. "Kneel, slut," Diego said and I did. He was opening me and lighting matches. He was prying me apart and putting burning matches near my skin.

"What are you doing? Diego, you're burning me." I was frightened.

"I'm looking for tape worms. You're a filthy boy," Diego drank a beer and smoked a cigar. "Now I want to hurt you."

"Is this my punishment?" I asked, waiting for his belt. Candle wax. Scalding water.

"Are you mentally deficient?" Diego laughed. "This is your reward."

I was on my knees. Night. My forehead on cool silk. My infant, untended, in a ring box. Then Diego changed his mind. He sat down on his side of the bed. He ordered me onto the floor, on my knees. "I can't trust the contamination," he said. "Just your mouth. Open."

Below, San Francisco was spreading herself, revealing her avenues of inflammation, taunting one to kiss, here above the harbor and the lamps. The sky and bay were identical, smooth, uninterrupted. I thought, simultaneously, of trespass and grace.

Below was the channel running under the Golden Gate Bridge out to the current and China. In the harbor, an elaborate choreography of sailboats, ferries, and ships carrying rumors and corrupted cargo. In a port city, it's a perpetual plague year. The ships might carry a pestilence that isn't even named yet. Malaria. Diphtheria. Influenza. It could be inside the crates of rancid fruit that spoil the air, or spill from carcasses in the holds, making gulls die, making tuna and halibut go away.

Diego stretched out on his back, a beached sea mammal. Beneath his alegría, his bonhomie, was an intrinsic sadness. Somewhere within his immensity, it was dusk and chilling and the door was locked, precisely as he expected. I was his point of entry. I was integral to this landscape, this portscape. The sea washed me in. I was all women with lacquered fingertips. All women with the

names of saints and jewels who stand at windows with golden wedding bands glowing like beacons in lighthouses. In a port city, all
women are dragon ladies, fire girls. They keep ships from drifting
off course. They keep men from drowning. This is why you pay them
in gold. They are expensive, but they can save your life.

I did not find the definitive tea set or a Buddha that illuminated itself and called to me. Perhaps I should have purchased the plate
with the severed heart and monkeys. Perhaps the carved cherrywood Buddha fondling a lotus. Would this have made our circumstances and how we interpreted them any different?

Diego completed his murals. I was often alone for consecutive
days and nights. I rode streetcars, crossed bridges, and smoked
opium in Chinatown. I spent storms with Jane, pulling out her hair
in handfuls like black mice or baby birds while rain fell on the fields
of window glass. We argued drunk, broke her antique furniture, and
ran through slicing wind to the store that sold opium behind the
tunnel and locked back door.

I painted. I read novels in English, and American newspapers
in cafés where people discussed politics with a frantic ignorance. I
went home with strangers. I went to hotels with people and did not
know their names. Did not ask. Was not told. I slid into their cars.
Or drew closer when they motioned with their fingers, brought my
ear to their mouth. Sometimes I charged money.

In December, I became a winter woman. December is notorious. Navigation is unreliable. Ships crash. A woman might make a
mistake. She might shoplift a sapphirine scarf from one of the new

department stores. A woman might put it around her neck and keep going. That is how grown-up children play. You see the door and open it, walk out to Union Square. The scarf? You've had it for years. Your husband bought it for you on Fifth Avenue in New York. It was afternoon. You ate cold chicken and pears in your hotel suite with a view of a brick courtyard, with a bench painted white against ivy. You remember absolutely. No one could question this.

I stole jewelry and gloves. I spent two days and a night in the opium room, having my pipe lit by a little boy who kept laughing. I rode cable cars. I smoked packages of cigarettes by the wharf. I went to shabby hotels rented by the hour with sailors, college boys, boys from farms who now drove trucks, boys who stacked crates and smelled of beer and ashes. The hotel rooms were faded teal floral wallpaper falling off and a single lightbulb hanging on a string, small, like a spider. I made them pay me one dollar. The walls were greasy and I ran my hands over what had once been bouquets and I licked my sticky fingers.

I went home with women I met in cafes near the museum or in bookstores. Once, a French woman, older than Mother. And several blond women with photographs of blond children they insisted I look at. Women who were married to Episcopalian lawyers from Philadelphia and Baltimore. They sported pointed felt hats with dark overly vertical feathers. They carried boxes embossed with the names of famous stores in New York and London and Rome. Women who were angry and liked it when I pulled my hair back like a man. I wore pants and told them my name was Rubén and they must call me this. I slapped and cursed them in Spanish and English, bits of Russian and French. I spit tequila on their bellies.

When it was too cold, when I had too much pain, I stayed in the apartment and painted. I would take Flora Violetta from the ring box. I let her crawl around the grooves in my palms, slide along my life and health lines. I put her in an ashtray so she could watch me work. I loved her absolutely.

It is San Francisco that is indelible. Diego is on the periphery. He had mistresses in the Anglo style, lean from tennis and knowing there will be enough money for their children and grandchildren, no matter who is president, no matter the outcomes of wars or stock markets, epidemics, inventions. Finishing schools sanded and polished them, encouraged their affection for horses. They became tedious. In between, Diego had his assistants who tended him, arranged food and wine, photography sessions, interviews with European newspapers, American magazines.

Our marriage quieted. I brushed my teeth and hair. I placed my ring box on the table beside the bed. I thought of Flora Violetta. Night was one seamless bolt of harbor-dark taffeta. It came in shades and strata, archeological, filled with petroglyphs on rocks. When I did sleep, I had nightmares.

Pain again, in my back and legs. My own earthquakes in abrupt shifts and spasms. Nelson Rockefeller sent special doctors to me. I received more surgeries. Was San Francisco the city of nine separate operations? I was sealed in casts with metal plates on the sides. It was like wearing knives. Sometimes I refused to speak for weeks.

I realized that the mute could talk. It is not that they lack the facility. But they have been taken by surprise. Their mouths are crowded with iris and slivers of rose. If they opened their mouths, gardens would pour out, rivers and oceans. Their voices are harsh, riotous. They have an edge which is frightening. Their offerings are rejected. Sometimes their lips are sewn shut with wire. Then they become clairvoyant.

Someday I would paint this juncture of intelligence and destiny. I would refuse to paint apples and pears and violins dissected into cubes. I would paint a stunted woman, startled to be found out, shocked to have survived. It was an experience to render in the delirious oranges of carnivals and influenza midnights near foreign ports.

Later, in Detroit or Chicago, Diego would point at his murals, as if they needed further amplification. "Frida, consider the scale. Look at the enormity." He would spread his arms out in triumph. "Compare this to what you do. You might as well be knitting. Your miniatures. They are less than postcards."

"That is true, Diego," I answered. "But they are postcards from another world."

Were we in San Francisco two years or three? I learned it is irony that makes the women fabricate their cashmere-and-cream smiles. Irony makes their skin mother-of-pearl. They become amphibious. Water women, drifting through ports beneath warships and yachts. I had become an autumn and winter woman, a water woman, a wind and bridge woman, with my baby daughter curled inside a ring box I carried in my purse. I had the solace of unde-tected betrayal. When Diego and I left San Francisco, I wasn't alone.

There was a sequence of events like separate symbols that form an equation designed to resolve the nature of love. If these hieroglyph-ics, sequence/event x symbols = love were inked into your wrist, they would form a permanent bracelet. The Nazis mastered these techniques. I have seen such markings on Jewish survivors of con-centration camps.

And I am etched with muddy slate lake residues. Detroit. Dirty as little-girl secrets. They will hide their panties under pond stones. They'll throw them away at the train station, on the tracks, or in the vacant field nearby, don't worry.

Then the death of my mother, foul-matted bird, oily and stiff with piety. The sub rosa births of my daughter, Flora. The ren-dezvous in New York and what should have been the culmination, Diego's affair with my sister Cristina. In between were galleries and museums, art schools, universities, villas, penthouses, airplanes, parades with marching bands offering songs of revolution. Women mink-trimmed and gloved and fuck you, I want more tequila. Hashish. Sleeping pills. Can I buy opium in Detroit? And isn't there something faster and more potent?

Only Flora Violetta mattered. Flora and my initiation into the art of vanishing. This is how you paint without canvas. This is how you create self-portraits that have nothing to do with you.

Morning or some approximation. Pebbles flung at the sides of the house, round and glassy as stones that mimic planets. Or clouds being gutted, gritty sand falls from their bellies onto the roof. They are dropping their babies.

Diego arrives with my ritual morphine. Not my Demerol. Just the prescribed morphine. Nurse with the syringe follows, a different kind of supplicant. We have to pay her. So it is morning?

"All night you told fabrications," Diego begins. "San Francisco. I was with you constantly. It was you who took a mistress. The Chinese girl who addicted you to opium. I permitted this. I was enlightened. You were not chattel."

"I was a seal balancing a ball. I was a zoo. You made me perform," I remember. I have lived through the night.

"You were undisciplined, Frida. Delinquent," Diego points out. "Reckless. Insane."

"You encouraged me. You insisted." I reach for my cigarettes, light one.

"You forget the milieu. It was prehistoric. People thought a match and a sack of pintos was a good time. Besides, it was good for business. We sold paintings. You called me Papa. You sat on my lap in your school uniform. You would unzip my pants with your teeth, beg me to show you Papa really loved you." Diego looks out the window, past the veranda, the garden and lime fountain.

Squalid morning, already steaming, tarnished, discouraged. They call this summer.

"Was I worthy," I want to know, "in love and war?"

"You were in all ways superior," Diego has considered this. He has an immediate response. "You were a better painter and you had more stamina. You were more refined and brutal."

"More intelligent, more imaginative," I suggest. "More daring."

"Without doubt. Your cruelty was inspiring. Ferocious. Relentless. I was continually entertained. You challenged me," Diego concludes.

"We had honor," I remember. "We did not lie on canvas."

"We were purified by the work," Diego is certain.

"Give me," I demand, my arms are canals. Now we must feed what lingers in the stale dawn, a sudden swarm of blind fish, mouths like night wells. "We'll talk after."

"You'll sleep after," Diego says, agitated but resigned.

Diego lacks an appreciation for the vagaries of vignettes. He believes there are indisputable memories, like chemistry formulas. He is convinced that progress is a matter of patterns, geometries that become buildings. I leave him with his ignorance. I just need him to tell Nurse to put the morphine in. Yes. Now.

I don't need a mouth. Morphine clarifies the memory, purifies and distills it, finds what was vivid, the indelible traces. With morphine a woman can find her footprints and follow herself down streets she does not remember. Startling images grow in the partial fish-silver dark, sulfur tinted, and singed like the aftermath of fireworks above a squalid river.

I was Diego's rare black pearl. Who knows how he found me? I explained mythology, which deities must be taken seriously, which to avoid when you are thirsty or have been disgraced. He described whorehouse practices with a rubbed-raw whiskey voice I mistook for authority. I became Diego's pet monkey, the one who played the organ while he passed his wide-brimmed fat man's hat around, while he spun his silver-plated pistol, waiting for dollars and commissions to be dropped in. I was his private carnival on display. I made the rumors dimensional. He insisted. Weren't we becoming rich?

"No one wants to attend opera anymore," Diego pointed out. "Now everyone wants to be an opera."

I was his terminal gypsy, his slice of rainforest, his parrot who said fuck me in the ass in six languages. His orchid who whispered, I love you, kissed his lips, and left the party with a young sculptor or poet. I held hands with women on pale brocade sofas on Fifth Avenue. I went for a walk and came back three nights later. I wore strands of beads with glassy surfaces like crystal balls. I was the future Diego held on a cord. I was his onyx, his anomaly.

The newspapers came. Photographers. We were stylized and recognizable. You could see us across an airport, a hotel lobby, and the plaza of a church. You could recognize us in any capital halved by a soiled gray river. We were better than vaudeville, smarter than Garbo, more exotic than Dietrich. They were strictly Old World,

European. They took cabaret seriously. We didn't need a script. When we opened our mouths, Freud and Marx, Kafka and Einstein and Picasso tumbled out. Monet, Miro, Ezra Pound, Hemingway, T. S. Eliot, Duchamp, Edward Weston, and Virginia Woolf. When they saw us on a boulevard, everyone knew the circus was in town.

Diego was painting a mural at the Detroit Institute of Art. He worked feverishly. He had taken a commission for the Rockefeller Center in New York City. The following year he had a commission for the World's Fair in Chicago. " I cannot play with you as usual," Diego said. He gave me a stack of money. "Run along. Pretend you are American. Buy."

Detroit was nothing like San Francisco, with its harbor and smell of coffee, bread, and cinnamon. Detroit was a riot of factories and brick and the limited palette of the last strangled century. This was the interior of the machine, gnawing on itself, going into a visual seizure that was rust, derelict corners, boards across buildings, dark children who looked starved, grave. Metal grids, iron bars, sharp points, wires that fenced and sliced the air. Even the sky seemed plowed and used. Here I felt the lure of alleys. Trains. Vagabonds. Women showing their shoulders and selling paper flowers. Pigeons. Beggars with flags. Jugglers. Men playing clarinets and trumpets with a hat at their feet in which one was supposed to toss coins.

It was a city of grays and browns, stenciled, somber. I was the only woman alone on the monotone boulevards. Everyone else was working in factories or was inside tending children I sensed were sick. I heard their cries through the brick and the boiling potatoes.

Then the season of American holidays began, each one alien and contrived. They came in a string like knotted ropes nuns once whipped their backs with. It began with mutilated pumpkins. Then the ritual slaughter of turkeys and baby pines. I stepped on leaves in the Detroit autumn. Later, snow made me isolated and morose. I had journeyed too far north. I felt the strain of my passage, the Casa Azul abstract now, the garden, the sly vines, moss, and how this had defined me.

Flora Violetta's hair would be like espresso. It would have the sheen of dark coffee beans, their oiled luster. In cafes above harbors, she would quote art critics, literary theorists, and the slogans of revolution. Revolution is seasonal. Flora would have hers with young men who sketched, played guitars, and pretended to be scoundrels. Young men with long hair, beards, and proletariat shirts. Flora would have an innate capacity for silence and the poetry of hell.

"You don't bring me lunch baskets anymore," Diego seemed to realize. He studied the area near the art institute wall, as if he might find a braided-ribbon offering of fruit and delicacies in a corner, wrapped in shadows. "No more breads on yellow flowers? No cherries? No chocolates?"

"I am busy painting," I answered.

"Do you paint? Or do you just fuck?" Diego was angry about the absence of lunch.

"Does it matter?" I asked.

"The men annoy me," Diego admitted. He was wearing his Stetson hat that day. He was wearing his ridiculous silver-plated pistol. "The women I understand. They are irresistible. But you cause me grief when you fuck my friends."

"Grief is not enough," I said. "I need you to remove body parts. Organs. I want your thumbs."

We laughed and kissed. Henry Ford and his son, Edsel Ford, were having a party for us that night. "I'm going to ask Henry Ford if he is Jewish," I told Diego. Diego was smiling as I left.

I walked on streets of oaks throttled with burgundy. Then an avenue of maples the yellow of distilled almond. I wanted to pull leaves off and suck them. Or stitch them into a cloak. This would be a baby blanket for Flora. I might need to protect or camouflage her.

"Conditioned properly, they will last ten thousand years," Diego announced, as if he were being filmed for a documentary. We were standing with Edsel Ford and the mayor. Edsel Ford and the mayor exchanged glances and nodded their heads, signifying awe and comprehension. Diego surveyed the walls of the Detroit Institute of Art, as if he were peering directly into the limestone. "Fifty thousand years." He reconsidered, "One hundred thousand years, if maintained to the letter."

I laughed behind my hand. My teeth were softening. A charcoal stain on one frail front tooth spread to the others, and my whole mouth suffered a contagion. I had begun to laugh out the side of my mouth, or with a fist across part of my face. I con-

cealed my teeth now, chewed tobacco, smoked additional cigarettes and a cigar.

Poor Diego, I thought, while a photographer appeared and
Edsel Ford shook his hand. What an idiot. Cities wouldn't last ten
thousand years, much less the murals on walls of a single building.
Cities were a failed experiment. Thebes. Constantinople.
Tenochtitlán. In ten thousand years, they would build machines to
do remedial labor. There would be electric progress one could not
begin to imagine. It was an obscenity to even speak of the shape of
this. It made Diego absurd.

"No one will know the word Detroit in ten thousand years.
It will be unpronounceable." I said. Lost as some village in the
mountains Genghis Khan passed through, had a son or two, a clay
vessel of wine, stole the horses, the young women with even
white teeth, and burned the rest down. No one speaks the name
of this village. It has been erased. There might be no cities at all.
Perhaps there would simply be instantaneous fluid monuments of
atoms and thought.

"But there will be cars," Diego laughed. He gave Edsel Ford
his endearing husband-of-the-sick smile and put his arm around
me. He bent down as if to kiss my cheek and whispered in my ear,
"Shut the fuck up."

I considered Diego's indios pulling corn from the land.
Perhaps in new cities corn would grow on the bottoms of oceans
or in greenhouses on Mars. Edsel Ford left the courtyard, then
the mayor.

"Do you learn this crap in American magazines for women?" Diego asked, still half searching the ground for his basket of strawberries set on branches of bougainvillea that wasn't there.

"Diego, you're becoming obsolete to me," I said with sadness. Then I turned and walked away. I could still walk.

In the skinned light of late afternoon in Detroit, in a fine strained lavender that made me think of prophecy and redemption, I imagined my unborn daughter. Flora, a confederation of browns like the sable of new paintbrushes, wheat breads, and the polished woods of pianos, and antique tables. And the fur-trimmed velvet opera cloaks in European novels. Flora would smell of flannel and seaport air and a stinging winter spice, nutmeg perhaps.

In the hotel room, I removed Flora Violetta from my ring box. In bed, with my knees raised, I carefully pushed her back into my womb. She nested in a crevice beneath my left hip where the metal rod had entered my body. I felt her breathing, a bold pulse. I could feel the throb of her lungs when I touched the folds of my skirt. I painted my face. I telephoned Henry Ford, asked him to send me gardenias and lilies for my hair.

"You are not pregnant," Diego said. "It is a physical impossibility."

He was eating steak. It was all he could trust in this city, meat and potatoes. The lake fish were bland and tough. Diego analyzed the defects of the menu while he drew slow circles on his belly. He was singing a lullaby to himself without using words. He was telling himself he was a good boy. He could have dessert. He could have two or three.

"I feel my baby," I revealed.

"You are delusional," Diego said, employing his schoolmaster voice. His bishop voice, which could foretell. "Perhaps you should paint more. It is unlikely, but you might improve. You could bring me lunches on the scaffolds again. It made you happy. And they were aesthetic, well composed. What do you do all day?"

"I walk," I told him. "With my baby growing inside." I lit a cigar. Tree stumps grew in my mouth. As I slept, blood trickled from my gums.

"What do you expect to find?" Diego seemed mildly interested. "Dragging your withered leg? Preying on strangers? Flaunting your calamities? You disgust me."

Diego considered the dessert cart. His concentration was a sustained intensity. I could see his internal machinery, the calculations. I was drinking tequila for dinner. Flora loved it. Diego was still engrossed by a variety of cakes. I may have broken a plate. Perhaps we were escorted from the restaurant.

A light dust of snow. I thought of cellos and how burning mesquite lingers in the high desert in winter, and how I would dress Flora in velvet with lace trim at the neck and cuffs. I would put baby pearls around her throat. I would take her to the ballet in every city. In darkness, we would hold hands, and I would memorize her bones.

In Detroit, with the baby Diego did not believe in, with the daughter he contemptuously dismissed, I began to practice vanishing. It came to me of a piece, the way a painting or a musical composition suddenly appears. It was like a trolley car collision. Then everything changed.

Cristina, a pale novitiate with a lace-covered silver tray. A pink bud in a vase. Cristina, face grave, drawn tightly like Mother. Stiff. She has bones that will fracture. Brittle bones. She will fall, break her hip, her skull. She will die alone in a 2 A.M. hallway.

"Is it still the same day?" I ask.

"It is the next day. Your fever was one hundred and five. You coughed up a basin of blood. Please stop smoking," Cristina says, makes two fists of her hands, and looks thrashed.

"What do you want?" I open my eyes. No sun. Is it night? It's a vestibule of pewter. Is it Henry Ford's house for Christmas dinner?

Coughing. It starts in the erasure where I once had toes. A spasm inside my thigh. But I don't have toes. They've fallen off. They were just glued-on stumps.

I light a cigarette. "Is it my birthday?"

"Not yet, Frida. Or always." Cristina is angry. "Every day is your birthday," She spits, bitter. O bitter bitter buttercup.

She pours herself a brandy, paces. "You know everyone," she continues. "The Rockefellers. The Fords. André Breton. Marcel Duchamp. Picasso. All the stars. Dolores del Rio. Joan Crawford does your toenails and licks the paint off. Noguchi cut off half a finger for you. Edward Weston takes your photographs. And Leon Trotsky. You are international."

"To know everyone is to know no one," I realize. So that is the emptiness, sad, so sad.

"You're starting to sound like Diego." Cristina, pale with rage.

I laugh. I do not bother to hide my mouth. I have four teeth left. Four logs of burned firewood. I won't survive the winter. Nurse has been to see me. I close my eyes, rock and drift, rock and drift.

"What do you want?" I ask Cristina.

There is a pause. In this juncture are the tanagers, the hummingbirds above peonies, the nights of thunder when the house sways. We are children again, holding hands in the garden near hibiscus and iris. We embrace our dolls, kiss them, feed each other berries. That was before Diego gave us both syphilis.

"Do you know what is next?" Cristina asks. Ashen face, poor dear, so expectant.

"Yes," I reveal. "Yes, I do know."

"Tell me," Cristina begs, reaches out, takes my cigarette. "Christ, Frida. You burn holes in Mother's blankets. You'll burn the house down. Tell me. What's next?"

"No." Who is she? Did I meet her on a street, on a trolley car? Did I meet her at a party at Nelson's weekend house? Or perhaps a brothel? I don't like the voice, vacillating between agitated and cloying. Leave me alone.

"But you'll tell me soon," Cristina says. "While you still can." This was the daughter Mother called graceful.

"Go to hell, Cristina."

"You first," she manages.

I laugh. She laughs. We embrace. Rock and sway. Cristina leaves a glass vial on the tray. Rock and drift. Rock and sway.

I could vanish. A vanishing woman develops unique navigational skills. A vanishing woman refuses official maps. It takes years to learn where to buy French bread and chocolates, fresh fish and lamb, pears, and who sometimes carries mangoes and papayas. Stores come into possession of the tropical without warning. Crates arrive in darkness like contraband. An inconspicuous hand-printed sign in the window. Mangoes, one day only. A woman who is vanishing notices this as other women would fire.

I limped in light snow, thin right leg behind me like an obscene afterthought. Morning was vague, a collusion of citrus and some essence from sheets women have hung in winter sun, a moist lingering. I felt vulnerable, a single partial glance could shatter me. One mistake and I could become the old woman in a wicker rocker on a veranda, making a list of the chances I'd missed, pushing thick air with swollen fingers, clutching a soiled pleated paper fan with a picture of a woman by a river with barges and cherry trees. A souvenir from Chinatown, perhaps. One misstep and I could be an arthritic woman with a sewing box stuffed with cheap trinkets, two spools of thread, matchbooks from marginal restaurants, and the ghastly remnants of holidays, party hats, and handfuls of moldy confetti.

By spring I couldn't walk. My leg was too heavy and leaden. Even brandy tasted tainted, metallic. There would be more hospitals, I felt this coming. Drilling or sawing, carving or stitching. I sensed this as women with bone and lung diseases can predict rain.

It was a spring of surgeries. I was confined to bed, to the bed Diego did not often return to. He was a soldier of fortune. Some commissions require removal of all garments. Penetration of orifices is often necessary. And props, white camellias and champagne. After all, Diego thought in terms of tens of thousands of years. He thought his murals on art institute walls in dreary already decaying inland cities would last longer than empires.

In between, I drank tequila until I collapsed in bed or on the floor near my paintings. It was a cold that wanted to teach me a lesson. It was a personal whiteout. I almost went blind. Swan Lake. Ballerinas with gauzy swan skirts swirling hip to thigh, now and gone. The edges stalled orchid white, dawn or dusk, who could decipher this? Tundra. I floated on sheets of ice, waiting for the next procedure, the next attempt to correct the last failure. I waited for the next hospital. Hospitals are the same, in capitals or villages. They are like airports or bus depots where you wait, but the loudspeaker does not announce your flight or destination. Hospitals are a terminal, the stakes are your life, and you leave in a wheelchair or a coffin.

In the hospital, I understood what vanished people value.

They believe in the sanctity of holidays. They are on the periphery, after all. The great-aunt. The best friend. They are what swells the crowd on Cinco de Mayo and the Fourth of July. There could be no decorations, no wreaths, party streamers, or piñatas without them. They are the mass on which headlines march. They are throwing confetti on the dock when your ship sails. They are waving banners in the rain and blowing party horns. They are the body count.

"What's the matter with you?" Diego complains. "You don't move anymore. You don't change your robe. You don't bathe. Are you molting?"

"I'm too busy," I answer

It must be between hospitals. I am in the hotel in Detroit. Autumn outside. Trees are henna, burgundy, and claret. It's a season for alcoholics and drug addicts. Women who smoke opium and collect divorces, run red lights drunk, feeling themselves coming apart like the landscape in a brutal confusion of russet and amber.

"Are you planning new paintings?" Diego is pale and, I suddenly realize, afraid.

"I am planning, yes," I say, not yet drunk.

"Where are your paintings? Meager and inconsequential, vulgar as they are. Frida. They are primitive, but where are they?" Diego opens a closet. He slams the door shut. "So you've hidden them?" Diego decides. "They're a travesty. But they occupy you, my dearest love."

"I've transcended canvas," I inform Diego. "I'm working in a region of absence."

This is not a lie. Rather, it is an approximation. Marriage is an exchange. Our lives as we perceive them, in their multiplicity, lack absolutes. We give each other rough estimates, sketches. We try to aim in the right direction. When our pathetic vignettes are recognizable, we say we are happy. When we are discovered in our fraud, we proclaim ourselves victims. The line between contentment and slicing a wrist with a razor is nonexistent.

The border between late white night and early white dawn in Detroit. I am curled in our bed, in my dragon lady red silk robe, smoking, drinking rum, drinking brandy, drinking vodka, and vanishing. The disappeared know all the shortcuts. They have an intuition for the physical plane, how a sharp left turn down a mile of cobblestone alley followed by a climb of six unexpected steep steps is faster than fifteen minutes in a taxi. The disappeared know where the carvings are, the buried frescoes, the stolen and lost museum paintings, and the doubloons from sunken galleons. Waves across rotting wood in which gold is contained is unmistakable. The vanished have an ear for this. They can tune into the precise frequency. It's like a radio channel.

Detroit, late autumn or early winter. I became more proficient. I comprehended scent and skin and their conjunction. And the gradations between bronze and peach, how they form a scale with nuances of tone. This can be played. Composition is possible. I opened bottles and heard flutes, Maríachis, and the metal rigging on ships in wind that is like tambourines.

I drank whiskey for breakfast. I squeezed oranges into my brandy. I understood fluid measurements and what they imply. Tactile information. I accommodated gracefully and synthesized. My fingers were conductors. Once I completely disappeared, there would be no more ruined spine, dislocations, loss of balance, mouth reeking. When I disappeared, symmetry would be trivial. There would be no more mistakes. I would be whole in absence.

I was released from the Henry Ford Hospital. Diego took me home, with balloons and champagne and fraudulent cheer. He kissed me, propped up my pillows, chitchat. How festive he was, placing roses in a vase, mentioning he had to leave for Chicago. He had already packed. He had a coat trimmed with fur at the neck that J. P. Morgan had given him spontaneously, a generous gesture. He had his Stetson hat, his pistol in his coat pocket. A bottle of brandy had been placed on the table near the bed.

Then Flora Violetta was born. She was a winter baby. Winter daughters are most prized, with their pearl-and-cream skin, their cheeks apricot, and how they long to be held. Winter daughters crave a mother's lap. They are indoor children, content with paints and poetry books and music. Often winter daughters play string instruments, choose not to marry, and remain with you.

I drank brandy, listened to the radio. I walked as if I were on a ship and I enjoyed this. I found a meat knife. I took my sharpest palette knife. I sterilized them in boiling water. When I completed vanishing, geography would open. I would sense emerging trade routes, ports and villages, and where to buy real estate. I would be famous for the acuity of my investments. I would charge consulting fees. I would tell everyone Detroit was useless, a waste of brick, a metal swamp. It would not last another hundred years. Detroit stank. Detroit had gangrene. Detroit should be amputated.

Flutter like a trapped bird. I was in my bed in the hotel suite with my knees spread and raised. I had folded my red kimono with peonies and tiny dragons embroidered into the silk. I had prepared the nursery. I had a music box lined with velvet and a dime-size sachet for a pillow. A lace handkerchief that had belonged to my father's grandmother. Her first blanket.

I was disappearing into the unexpected. The eight-year-old girl downstairs was playing a Chopin nocturne with lethargic cruelty. Foghorns and bells formed a sequence. They were points of light you could plot on a graph or paint. I would like to paint Diego in the park near the Institute of Art. A shabby park littered with denuded oaks and lindens. Diego thought them accidental. He didn't think about them at all. He didn't realize that he was the white-haired man alone near the fountain with the stale croissants. If Diego bothered to glance from his scaffolds across the frayed trees ringing the city park, he could have seen himself.

I inserted the instruments. They were insignificant, after the metal handrail, after the collision had already rearranged the proportions of my body, my female cavity. I took a deep breath. Then I dug in, made slow grooves, sharp eddies, circular gulfs. I was looking for Flora with metal.

A man and woman were comparing Diego to Picasso. They were whispering.

"They are defined by their treatment of women. Pablo takes pleasure from the torment of females. He is deliberate. He searches for victims and novel methods of inflicting pain," the man said.

"I met a woman he bedded. She showed me the scar where Pablo put out a cigarette. He called her his ashtray. He made her beg for the burn," the woman said.

"I heard that story," the man agreed. "Pablo claimed it was not a scar, but a brand. An emblem of immortality."

"Rivera is more casual. He isn't premeditated. He's convinced the suffering of women is an inevitability, like sexual attraction and the decay of age," the woman explained.

"Picasso is a misogynist. His women with sharp cuts on the skin. The brutal slashes on their faces," the man decides.

"But Rivera is more devious," the woman says.

"How is that?" the man asks, surprised.

"Diego views women as calla lilies and fruit. Bovine. Still lifes. Something to eat," the woman says. They laugh.

"And look at that woman, that Frida. The pathology," the man says. He is breathless.

"It's depravity," the woman decides.

They walk away. The gluey light. The gray at the corners of the room, pools of dusk on the floor. I sleep. Later, I hear the doctor say, "It's worse than you think."

It is the Henry Ford Hospital in Detroit, Michigan. Diego, the pragmatist, that soldier of expanding good fortune, the mercenary of art, said, "How could it be worse?"

"It wasn't a natural hemorrhage," the doctor informs him.

Diego defends me. The tone of his voice resists. They are standing near my feet. My eyes are still closed. "She is deformed from the bus accident," Diego says, gallantly, defiantly.

"It's not that," the doctor explains, his words sharp, precise, a flock of gleaming scalpels in the too thick hospital light. In the corridors, golden moths with metal mouths. They feed in hospitals and depots. They spread infection. They carry cancer. They slip through the mesh. They bite you as you brush your hair at dusk and you develop insomnia. "It's self-inflicted. We're certain. She did it to herself," the doctor says.

"But it would have taken hours," Diego points out. He sounds like he may start screaming.

They kept me in the hospital for weeks. Diego was enraged. "Why become insane in Detroit?" he would repeat, enjoying his wit, smoking cigarettes, and pacing the perimeter of the hospital room. "New York, Paris, madness is plausible there. It is unthinkable in a city such as this. They only know about cars here."

I sleep because I am sedated. They give me morphine. They approve of my lassitude, they decree it. A statement is issued saying that I, Frida Kahlo, wife of Diego Rivera, have had a miscarriage. When I wake up, I am hysterical. "Lies. They're telling lies,"

I cry. Then they inject me, and I fall through the earth, into a well of lilac and orchids in a Mexican dusk.

They are wrong. I will take Flora back into my womb and return to Mexico. I will give birth in the Casa Azul, where I can hide and protect her. In darkness lit by the eyes and mouths of golden moths, I put my daughter back inside me, piece by piece. I had been concealing her in my slipper. I am an autumn woman, a master of camouflage and concealment. Flora pops back in.

They wanted me in the hospital longer, but death interferes. My mother's death. I returned to Mexico for her funeral. It was an entirely ceremonial occasion. Mother had already become a rubbed-away charcoal sketch to me. She had receded into the background, along with the forests you pass only once and too quickly on a train, the bridges you glimpse behind ridges of pine and forget. Mother had taken her place along with all the accumulations of the periphery. She was a woman wearing gloves and pearls at a gallery, she might buy a canvas, and one was polite. She was conversations with strangers in hotels. She sat on a park bench making predictable chatter about Communism, and evil, and the cinema. She poisoned the afternoon.

"Stop it, Frida," Cristina said, eyes fierce, mouth smeared with lipstick half rubbed off. "You can't smoke at a funeral." Cristina, pulling the cigarette from my hand, stamping it out on the dirt. She hadn't gotten syphilis from Diego yet. Now Cristina wants to know what comes next. Should I tell her?

Mother was consigned to the undifferentiated static with saints I had forgotten. Who guarded sailors and women with malaria? Who watched over lovers and lepers? Who cured fevers and broken bones? Who rationed illumination and absence?

After the funeral, I gave birth to Flora. I lived multiple lives so I was allowed more than a single birth. This time it was normal. It happened in the back garden. I was kneeling in earth, in a row of peppers and strawberries, and my infant floated up from the dirt like a translucent female lily. Night was a calyx. I wrapped Flora Violetta in my father's grandmother's handkerchief. A spasm under lace. I hid her in my purse and told no one.

"What's wrong with your feet?" Cristina asks. Has she slept with my husband yet?

"I don't know what you mean." Dimwit. I am hurried. Flora is in my purse, in a handkerchief with initials embroidered on both sides. She is hungry. She needs to be fed strained food. I will give her rice and poppies.

"You don't take your shoes off. You sleep with your shoes on," Cristina is observant, assured. She believes she can read a compass but she can't even see Flora.

"My toes are bruised," I begin.

"Your bruises. Your operations. Your love affairs." Cristina is outraged. "In New York, they talk about your surgeries at theater intermission. In Paris they gossip. Your sickness makes you famous."

"Fuck off," I say. Flora is hungry. The morning isn't long enough. "Jump in the dirt. Keep Mother company."

"Do you think disease buys you forgiveness?" Cristina asks.

"Forgiveness?" I open my mouth in wonder. I breathe in acres of lightbulbs and moths. "Forgiveness isn't even on my map." The taxicab came.

I am near the airport. Then I realize Flora has no passport. I lack signatures and documents. Diego is waiting for me in New York, angry and threatening. He's left messages. The newspapers will be waiting. I felt the pin on the hand grenade in my head being pulled.

"Stop," I say. The taxicab stops.

It is an arcade or fair. No, it is the plaza of a cathedral crowded with people and burros and oxcarts, dogs. It's a market for people from the provinces. They have set up booths with fabrics for doors. They are selling carvings and beads, gourds in the shape of fish, mantillas, blankets, and old saddles. Noon is blistering. My skin feels like it's being peeled off.

She is fat. Her feet are swollen, ankles wrapped in bright rags. She wears a straw hat, brim uneven from rain. A belt buckle of brass in the shape of a fish. Her burro has bells around his neck. Her jaw curves where it has been broken. One eye is a watery pink from infection. Is this the one? Is she distinctive? The glare. The taxicab waiting.

"What is your name?" I ask. "How old are you? Where are you from? Your village?"

"I am María Elena Campos. I am thirty-one. I come from Córdoba, Señora." She has a child's voice. She smiles shyly, glances at my skirt, my necklaces. The taxicab honks twice.

I ask if she has children. She says no. She had two sons but they died in the floods.

I take Flora out of my purse. I hold the handkerchief in my palm. "Do you know what this is?" I ask.

"It is for crying," María Elena Campos says, watching me with wide eyes. "And to breathe through when touching corpses."

"This is my daughter, Flora Violetta," I begin. "She is sleeping inside the lace. I don't have a passport for her. I need you to take care of her for a year. Maybe two years."

I explain Flora's special diet. Black beans and poppies. I rummage in my purse, count out American money. Seven thousand American dollars.

"You must return to this market," I tell her. "You must promise, every year. So I can find Flora. Do you promise?"

"I promise, Señora." María Elena is grave. She takes Flora from my hand, pauses, and places the handkerchief in her apron pocket.

"I want you to remember me," I say. I bend toward her. "Smell me."

María Elena places her nose near my face. I open my mouth. It's a scorched-dry arroyo. Something metallic, like tin. And cigarettes, pulque, coffee, and Marxist slogans. Medicines. Sea salt. My gums are gray and sticky. A new blister near my tongue.

"Will you remember?" I ask.

"I will remember you every day, Señora," María Elena Campos says. She produces a rosary and kisses it. "I will never forget you."

"I'll see you in a year," I remind her. We embrace. I close my eyes and breathe wet rope, barn, and disintegrating saddle leather. Then I turn and the cab door is open and we are moving.

We are riding to the airport. Out the window, women are selling fruit and blankets, fabrics with vivid geometries are still as if starched. Noon. No breeze. Burros, goats, dogs, children crouching in shadows because their feet are burned. Another church. Women dressed for death. Men with cigars, spitting and coughing. An alley with lepers missing hands. Nuns. Naked boys in a broken water pipe. Pigeons. Heaps of stones that have fallen or been abandoned where they are. Men selling ropes for horses, whips, and hats. Women offering melons, tamales. I tell the taxicab to stop. I limp in a slow circle around the vehicle, shading my eyes with my hands. I have no idea where María Elena Campos is.

I joined Diego in New York, curiously detached, stomach cramping with afterbirth. Diego had left a message with the pilot. He had written it down and folded it into an envelope. The pilot presented me the note, bowing with ceremony.

Newspapers will be on the tarmac. It's snowing here. Wear your Tehauna costume and flowers. Do not forget lipstick.

I drank too much on the airplane. I took pills for pain. I considered Diego's immensity, his unrelenting purpose. Didn't he realize I knew how to bury a mother without getting dirt on my dress? Didn't he sense I knew how to give birth and hide this in a leather purse? Didn't he suspect that I was in the process of vanishing?

"Your paintings are ugly," Diego would say.

"Not as ugly as life," I would reply. I was freeing myself as I painted. It was physiological. There was nothing abstract about it.

"You put too much in," Diego insisted.

"I don't put in enough," I would counter. The collision had liberated me from the dictates of ordinary symmetry. Perhaps symmetry was not necessary. It might even be an acquired taste. Balance might be the aberration.

"You're merciless," he would decide.

"I am gentle," I would answer. Poor Diego. My paintings were miniature but lethal, like eating glass or having it splinter in your fingers. It takes months for such cuts to heal.

Diego was installing a mural at Rockefeller Center. Later, he insinuated a portrait of Lenin into a scene. Then he refused to remove it. Diego did this deliberately to make Nelson Rockefeller angry. He thought it would generate publicity and it did. Diego was delighted. His name in newspapers fueled him.

"It is free advertising for future commissions," Diego cried out, his voice throttled with emotion. He might have been at a bull-fight. The public squabbling would continue all year. "Free advertising," he repeated, kissing the newspaper. I remembered Diego would put his mouth anywhere. All behaviors are contagious. You can be contaminated even as you sleep. That is why one must choose a husband with care.

On the streets bordering Central Park, it was a season of velvet party gowns trimmed with gold, high heels and triple strands of pearls. My Tehuantepec costumes were too thin. I complained to Diego, claimed the cold made me drink tequila. He bought me a mink coat. It was in a box on the bed.

"Be naked under it," Diego suggested. "Tell J. P. Morgan you'll keep the coat on. Say you're cold."

I did not bring Diego a lunch basket as he worked on the scaffolds at Rockefeller Center, preparing to sabotage his mural with a cameo of Lenin. Instead, I walked down boulevards where I did not shop, letting myself find smaller streets, narrow, unkept. I was moving away from hotels and department stores, from the Empire State Building and Central Park. I was finding derelict alleys where broken whiskey bottles were, overturned trash, yards with newspapers caught in barbed wire. I was clandestine. I smoked marijuana alone, in littered back streets. I followed alleys, peering into windows and over ripped wire fences, up unlit stairs of tenements reeking of onions and cabbage, garlic, red wine, and bad plumbing.

In apartments, women dried aprons and towels on iron railings in angular patches of frail winter sun. They had a parakeet in a cage, a bird called Coco or Daisy. Plastic sheets covered the good sofa where they rarely sat. Details accumulated and made decisions manifest.

In these rooms, women had photographs of grandchildren taped to chipped cupboards. A blond on a swing, trees that looked ripped, machine-gunned in the background. A man who might be a son squinting across a trimmed sad lawn straining to smile. A red-head with a six-shooter, face contorted with intensity. He was trying to turn the air to sulfur.

These could be photographs of anyone's grandchildren. After the harbors and plazas, trolleys and bridges, there were severings. These women with grandchildren three by five inches watch birds from their windows. Where do they go after this city? Do they navigate by lakes and rivers? The boy taped to the cupboard with his pistol and wide mouth cannot know her. How can these women be certain the images are not acts of fraud?

I limped through the lower edges of Manhattan, carrying a pint of brandy in my mink coat pocket. Liquid clarity. I realized that once you have disappeared, you recognize your connection to all women leaning on balconies in bathrobes with their caged birds and stringy starved plants. And women sitting in wicker rocking chairs on wooden verandas with a view of barbed wire and empty dirt lots where boys sharpen sticks in the dusk.

Partial vanishings are possible. A photograph of such women would show them as out of focus. Some women miss their coordinates, waver at crisis, and lose their nerve. Their vanishing is incomplete. They had the concept but failed to construct the necessary tunnels or devices. They could not deceive the border guards and the detecting machines. They did not comprehend what was required to procure forged documents, who to bribe, fuck, blackmail, or kill. They did not recognize the seriousness of the moment, its gravity like so much pewter, thickening the day, graying it.

I could determine which women had failed to devise a plan of contingencies. Their shadows leaked out of them. Their dreams were leached. All that remained was a triangle of December sun and bells in a distance that meant nothing. Such women inhabit the periphery of neighborhoods where languages they do not understand are commonly spoken. Russian. Polish. Yiddish. Chinese. They become women of the backwater ports. I thought, Frida, you must be careful this doesn't happen to you.

I took taxicabs to the apartment facing Central Park that Nelson had provided for us while Diego did his mural. I wore my new silk robe, a pale kimono with orchids stitched across a white so icy it looked like you could skate on it. I was an insignificant frozen lake. I was a place to spend an afternoon. My dragon robe had been thrown away after the hemorrhage we did not and do not speak of. It was not a miscarriage. That was Detroit, where I almost lost my daughter, Flora, with her seaport hair hanging like pelts down her back, and her sable eyes.

"You smoke too much," Diego said in New York.

I did not answer him. I didn't know what he was talking about. And the reply of one perpetually sick wife was insignificant. The invalid wife, but so photogenic. I was a complete political statement. The camera made me a manifesto, immaculate. Diego needed me, his three-dimensional amulet. And there was the matter of the family business, which we owned, the way a man and woman might a neighborhood tienda. Instead of tomatoes, beans, and beer, we sold canvases and ambiance. We sold style.

"You are forbidden walks," Diego said. "You're supposed to swim."

I was smoking and drinking wine. Vanished women are drawn to smoke. They are not afraid of fire. They consume two or three packages of cigarettes a day. They wear a variety of vermilion lacquers on their fingernails. They smoke opium from antique ivory and cloisonné pipes once used by the concubines of warlords. They paint their lips autumnal. Pacific sunsets, and aspects of maple. They know how sharp coral is. Their hands and mouths are lethal. They keep journals, diaries. They are not anxious at twilight or in the awkward gap before the lamps are lit. They draw illumination from air.

"You curl in the dark like a dying animal," Diego notes.

"It isn't dark," I say. He watches with distaste as I smoke. "And I am a dying animal." He ignores me, turns on lamps. He is satisfied by surface light.

There is no imprecision on the cusp between winter and spring. The zones surrounding seasons have their own identities, their barbed wire assurances. There are passwords, gestures vanished women memorize. The mid-December shift, the acceleration into fever and influenza. The air was gray. I did not need to consult my watch. It was the hour for intoxication. It was the hour of a single word. Opium.

Perhaps it was Christmas. I sensed it in the holly wreaths, the sweet burning cedar and profusion of elaborate ribbons. It was in the brandy. The essence of red, what turned it festive and indelible. The edges became elegant under a grainy pewter half-light thin as razors. We know ourselves in the damp beneath street lamps when we are waiting for strangers.

"You sleep all day," Diego accused. "Then you're awake all night, inventing curses. Making love to yourself on canvas. Why don't you sleep?"

"I'm waiting to fuck Santa," I said.

"Not the reindeer?" Diego smiled.

"I will gang-bang them. And the dwarves and elves, of course."

New York was opium in taxicabs before cocktail parties, dinners, and receptions. Diego was being feted, becoming larger while I disappeared.

My face was a composition. This time there would be no errors. I had the hands of a surgeon, a concert pianist, a serial killer. I painted what could not be spoken. I painted my face by a single nub of candle. I did not need light. I did not need a mirror.

"You have energy again," Diego noticed, evaluating his ties, holding them in his fingers, tenderly. Something about the opera or a patron at the theater. An important dinner, and yes, so sudden. He was overly hearty. I suspected he had a rendezvous with another heiress. She would be tailored, a woman of tweed and high boots who had recently returned from a tiger hunt in Hindustan and knew the king's brother.

I stared at my canvas Fridas, my paints, my small knives. I wanted to cut the wrist of winter. I wanted to bleed like a river in mist, under a siege of loitering maples, under their fleshy fists. In late December, you don't need headlights. You can navigate by the cries of babies deserted on the sides of roads, tossed into arroyos, left in alleys and plazas. Mouths like fish and unformed roses, opening, calling for Mama. I should send money to Flora's surrogate mother, María Elena Campos. I must make certain she has meat in winter. I have thousands of American dollars. But I do not have her address.

Diego was preparing for his infidelity. He smoked opium. Vodka in a crystal goblet on the ledge of the marble tub. Bubbles in the hot bath. Starched shirt. Radio jazz. In his shadow, inflamed stars burned down. He was killing the galaxy. I shot him with an arrow. Then I pulled the arrow out of his chest and shot him again.

"Why do you stare?" Diego was annoyed. "Why don't you just collapse, Frida? It's your stupor time. Try a coma."

There is no infidelity. We have multiple identities. There are increments of variation. It was New Year's Eve. I painted a face that was not my face onto canvas. I was solitude, distilled and refined. I was alone beneath reefs of constellations with their somber russet shells like uninhabited bodies of water abandoned as they slept.

The garish American holidays went into remission. I accompanied Diego to parties in country houses given by men who owned banks and fleets of ships and had boulevards named after their fathers. I made them laugh, gasp. They were aghast, but still amused. I drank whiskey. I mimed eating, moving carcasses of sea creatures across an English porcelain plate. I rarely ate. I was defining the constants. Betrayal, both planned and accidental. Heartbreak in an auburn dusk. A voice hoarse. Skeletons of chestnut trees. Then the itch of agitation you scratch like a rash until you break the skin with your nails.

Diego said, "You were brilliant tonight. What sly sabotage. You are my little flower. You are my charm. Sit on my lap. Then I'll give you a bath. I'll carry you to bed. I'll reward you until it hurts."

I had worn a Tehauna costume to this party. I had ordered gardenias and orchids for my hair. John said to call his florist whenever I wanted and I did. I had flowers even after Diego stuck Lenin in the mural on Rockefeller Center. Even after John fired Diego, I had a fragrant jungle perched on my scalp.

But that season Diego was drawn to the opposite. Cool women in sedate cashmere who wore cameos at their throats and one simple antique pin in their hair. I was a parrot woman, a piece of caged rainforest that had been taught to repeat a few obscene phrases and it does. Fuck me in the ass. Beat me with a buckled belt. OK. My turn.

We left New York and everyone was glad. We had worn out the welcome mat. We had bled on it, vomited on it, spilled tequila and put out cigarettes on it. A delegation accompanied us to the ship. They had bought our tickets and helped pack our bags. It was not a celebration. They wanted to ensure our departure. There were irate husbands and wives. They sensed we were a parasite, a corrosive that could consume anything.

Still, Diego resisted. "They're dismal and provincial. They're banal," Diego complained, "but they have so much." He was teary, slumped.

We departed on schedule. I must reclaim Flora. I would find María Elena Campos. María, with her swollen feet, her pink eye, her brass fish belt. María, with her drowned children and dead husband. She sold woolen blankets in the market in the plaza of the cathedral near the airport. Diego was morose, seasick. He drank and slept. He blamed me for our cabin, which he claimed was inferior in size and furnishings. He asked me for opium.

Diego was on his back, eyes half closed. He was naked. "Show me you love me with your whore's mouth," Diego said. I straddled him on the narrow ship bed. I put him in my mouth.

"It's no good," Diego said. "Put on lipstick. Thick and red. I'll imagine you're hemorrhaging."

"Will that be enough to excite you?" I inquired. We were playing.

"I will embellish. An enraged man has punched you in the mouth. You have a broken jaw," Diego smiled.

I painted my lips with layers of Dragon Lady. I smoked a cigarette. I smoked opium. When I returned, Diego had rolled over onto his belly.

"Straddle me," he said. "Spread me with your fingers. Pretend I'm a woman. Show me how you love a woman with your mouth."

"Go wash," I tell him. "You've haven't bathed for days."

"Shut up," Diego said. "Assume the position. And gentle, Frida. If you cut me, I will break your arm."

I painted My Dress Hangs There, in New York, in 1933. It is my Tehuantepec costume with white pleats at the skirt bottom. The dress hangs between a pedestal on which an American flush toilet gleams. On the other side, a gold trophy of the type given to athletes. I painted factories, a clock and a garbage can with body parts inside it. Then a church and a window where a dance hall girl in the style of Mae West stands while buildings below her are on fire.

"The political message," Diego smiled. "That is rich, Frida. That is magnificent."

"Politics are the least of it," I said.

He did not ask why only my dress was showing, a garment without a body. An uninhabited costume. He did not wonder where the woman who wore the dress was. For Diego, I had already vanished.

I am cold. After the small atrocities by lamplight, I remember the sea and the proportions of the heart. I am alone with my prophecies. It's been weeks of air and the solitude of deserted capitals where war has left nothing but church bells.

"Frida, please," Cristina begins.

"First Demerol," I say. "Is it the same second day?"

"It's the third day." Cristina turns on the lamp. A tray. Syringe. The faceted vials of Demerol. It has a sharper jolt than morphine. It's like making love with a razor.

I glance at my sister. I know what she wants. "Not yet," I tell her.

"What do you think about? Or do you just count the transgressions of others?" Cristina asks.

"You sound like Mother," I realize.

"Try to think of an hour when you were happy. Or a landscape. You said you never met a landscape you didn't like." She is holding both of her hands in her lap, squeezing and twisting her fingers together.

"Not yet, Cristina." I watch her walk slowly across my room. I pick up the glass and metal objects she has left me. Perhaps I will consider landscapes. After all, there is only earth and silence and trembling in all the ruined latitudes. We are bodies with hands, words, and longing in the nights of impossible gatherings beneath jacaranda trees. Then I hear Cristina close the door.

In heartbreak all streets look like Paris. Leaves like kissed mouths in gutters beneath lamplight and lindens. No rust, no metallic stains. Edges are smooth as if by tongues. Chestnuts are the texture of hypnosis, a quality similar to somnambulism but more curious, like waking in your sleep and drowning.

Diego and I have not yet divorced. I was given an exhibition in Paris. I traveled alone. The Louvre purchased what they mistook to be a self-portrait. It was titled The Frame. It was 1939. It was an astonishment. I, Frida, a primitive, an insignificant painter, sold a canvas to the Louvre. Frida, a triviality, a slut, a brazen misanthrope, the dirty-mouthed wife of Diego Rivera, was, for a moment, visible.

I had expected this only after my literal death. That is the way with women artists. When she is dead, she cannot harm you. Perhaps I was considered already dead. I had been living posthumously since I was seventeen.

The Frame is a painting in which the frame is central, my face barely of consequence. My act of heresy, my act of outrage at borders and traditions, had been accepted. The fools called it a self-portrait because they were critics without eyes. They were certain I was a narcissist. Or I was merely a Mexican woman making a decorative object like an embroidered pillow.

It is not a painting, but a scientific formula. It is a manifestation of vanishing, how a woman looks as she begins to disappear, as the periphery becomes more vivid, mysterious, and intricate than the woman herself, who is no longer fully there.

Alone in Paris I was startled awake. Trees seemed rinsed with henna, tinted with copper. And what was that one red leaf shaped like a small heart or a mouth? Don't tell me. I know. We are all waiting to be kissed or slapped. Air was the tantalizing cobalt you only see on airport landing strips at night, an infused predatory gleam, intelligent and throbbing. It was modern like atoms and pollution and army tanks. It could eat lilacs and harbor waves, babies, monuments in forests of mangrove.

The Bretons were tedious, their formality self-serving. I could barely keep from becoming instantly drunk. They made their servants curtsy. Bourgeois hypocrites. They deified knowledge. They thought their philosophy and symbology ineluctable.

Their chairs were hard. They let the dogs sleep on the sofa. Dog hair burned my eyes. I pinched a fingernail into my thumb to try to stay awake.

In Paris, I carried morphine and syringes, Demerol when I could contrive to find or buy it. I went into their bedroom and administered a large dose to make my mood more amiable. Then I had a second, to insure my decorum and wit. I returned to their hard chairs. They were still talking. André termed me a great surrealist. I denied interest in his movement.

"You don't understand," Jacqueline Breton began, as if I was from a tribe that had not yet invented language.

"You don't understand." I stood up. "You have the luxury of dream. These are rich people's parlor games. I have the reality of my disintegrating body." By midnight, in rage, I defined myself as a realist.

I limped into the night, slamming the door behind me. Later they told Kandinsky and Picasso that I had foul skin and offended them with my morphine. Picasso said he wanted to meet me. He telephoned me twice and I hung up.

I required taxicabs. I must be careful or I would be back in the wheelchair. I took taxicabs to parks, gardens, stretches of riverbank. Then I limped to a bench. Autumnal Paris rubbed my flesh and I walked until I felt my toe bones breaking like twigs. Then I would bandage myself and walk again while stains spread on my stockings. The stick, the moist flap of flesh, eggshells, pus. I carried rolls of gauze and wrapping tape in my purse near my morphine kit with syringe and tourniquet. I still had veins like airport runways. I could lean into myself, slip the tip of the syringe in, and no one by the river or in a park of elms and stone men on horseback noticed.

Fall. Damp leaves belly up in startlement. A litany of leaves like lipsticked mouths in gutters, what rustle, what taffeta, what October shudder. A canopy of branches had turned magenta, skinned bark a burgundy I could get drunk on. The parks were variations of auburn, charcoal, and russet. There was the fragrance of early lamplight, which is distinct like wild anise on northern riverbanks.

Solitude insinuated itself, courted and seduced me. Ferns emitted shoots like green darts and flares. I considered their primitive qualities. Even in extreme periods of austerity, it was rarely an empty mockery for me. The deranged are fully occupied.

She appeared from a brick building denoting itself as a residence for the elderly. I watched her walk on the boulevard, recognizing that her slow examination of the trees meant she understood them as talismans and relics. She sensed the implications. She possessed the facility for calculation and rapture. She stooped, picked up a leaf turned purple, an early fall causality. It was obvious. She was a vanished woman.

I followed her, an old woman wrapped in wool. A woman that radiated clairvoyance. She had deliberately divested herself of everything, thinned, knew silence as a caress. Aged women alone feel the orbit of the planet, how well oiled it is, how it spins, elegant and restrained. The celestial passage is filled with extravagant illuminations. Sunstruck maples and elms. Lamps glimpsed in strangers' rooms behind lace curtains, creamy as afterbirth.

Paris. Leaves fallen like upended boats with drowned women inside. Could she count the bodies in a maple leaf? There are five.

I imagined her voice would be that of a girl, eyes downcast and proper. Then she would startle with invectives in a voice harsh and brutal, as if she had swallowed winter wind. She had abrupt swings of mood, now elated, now sullen. Her children called her difficult. No one spoke to her in the home for the elderly. What circumstances, what failed intrigue, had deposited her here?

In a bakery, she let the moment of selection elongate. She bought her breads by aroma, by which seemed heaviest. There are acres of meaning between corn, rye, wheat, and pumpernickel. She chose a dark round loaf.

She turned her head from side to side, as if taking a temperature of her emotional climate. Was she frightened? Angry? Bereft? When she tilted her head, did she hear the planet on axis like so many metal wind chimes?

Women who have slept alone for decades in anonymous temporary rooms have entire solar systems locked within them. They have answers to questions about the value of religion in the midst of chaos and how to sustain faith. The vicissitudes of economies and families. Where the lines are between sanctity and fraud. They know, but no one asks them.

The woman rested on a bench in a miniature park near the river. Once she simmered stews and soups, turned the house dense with meat and onion, garlic and butter. This lingered on her. Now she glanced at the people nearby, a glimpse and she could measure their destinations and motives. She could determine pleasure from necessity.

She closed her eyes. I closed mine. We were connected. A bridge formed across the theoretical gulf that separated us. The bread pressed to her chest was still warm. I could feel it. I knew what widows think when they close their eyes in city parks. They consider varieties of soup and the availability of vegetables and fuel. They deliberately forget the names of their grandchildren. They erase the words for their favorite flowers, the titles of paintings and novels, and how to iron skirts. This particular vanished woman was counting the harbors and seas she had known, recalling precisely what made each distinct. They remember their lovers, a handful of enlarged mug shots.

Her body was oddly stilted, and her mouth rigid, fortified. It was not arthritis, but a stroke. Her speech had become awkward, unpredictable. Her lips were numb. Her children put her in a home for the aged against her will. They refused to sort out her meager syllables. She writes them letters that they reject as sentimental and inconclusive. They have no capacity for the language of her body, although she has become adept at pantomime. She was disappearing. Then she vanished.

Yes. This woman has an entire moral architecture. She knows why bridges and terminals fascinate. She has philosophical questions demanding a definition of human conduct. What is loyalty? What constitutes integrity? How is it distinct from circumstance? Her thoughts are undiminished. But it takes too long to assemble the words and hammer them out. Her tongue sits sullen in her mouth. Fat. A cold pewter tool broken, swollen, and resistant.

There were junctures where her life might have been completely changed. There was a seaside inn for sale. Wood. Green shutters. Fifteen windows facing the sea. They chanced to spend a weekend there. She had recently married Henri. He had a small inheritance. They might have purchased it. Stayed out of the city altogether. She could have breathed salt air, worn only straw hats and dresses of oyster linen.

It was a shallow bay. There would have been no tragedies. The bay by the inn was the texture of felt hats and certain wool coats popular that season. If they had stayed longer at that inn, and she had wanted to, had almost insisted, their whole lives would have been different.

Once she saw a for-rent sign on a carved wooden door. An opulent fern hung in the upstairs window above terra-cotta pots of geraniums. The room supported life. It asserted an opportunity to breathe. She could have rented that room, she had enough money. She could have rented that room and an entire other identity would have begun.

She had only to cross an avenue. She could ring the bell and change her name, procure new documents, invent a past. She could forget the house of onions and breads and children who would eventually discard her. She had only to touch her knuckles to the wood, which was more than a door. It was a passage. But she didn't. She could have vanished. She had the intuition for disappearing but not the courage.

I watched her walk into a fruit and vegetable market. The scent of fruit was a caress. The cool geometry of berries quickened her breathing. She experienced a thrill in the market, the anticipation of what would be on display, what sudden and inexplicable abundance.

One Thursday it was strawberries and snap peas. The shop was packed with them, as if a cargo ship had landed laden only with them. They were in burlap sacks on the floor, huge bamboo baskets, and crates. The store smelled of the country where she might have purchased an inn with a pear orchard, a trellis with purple clematis and wisteria and everything would have been different.

She held a pear in her hand. She studied the shadings of lime across its surface like antique brocade. She watched shadows make the aubergines appear rained on, slick, oiled, black. The old woman thought they looked painted, like still lifes in a museum. Or an ornament from antiquity locked in a glass case.

Flora Violetta would not condemn me to a home for the elderly, to a room without my dolls and carvings, beads and paints, my hidden vials of Demerol, my duplicate key to the morphine cabinet. Flora would read my lips. She would trace my mouth with her fingertips, close her eyes, and it would be as if we were actually speaking.

Later, I would hear her laughter. A sweet musicality. What was she doing? She was practicing making her mouth a well and kissing

KATE BRAVERMAN

in hallways of rogue shadows smelling of jasmine and opium. She
was practicing by kissing her arm.

I thought of all the women in markets across the continents
and I was racked with profound joy. Women, simultaneously clandestine and deliberate, contriving methods to determine freshness
and sweetness. Is it ripe? Will it last the week? Is it enough? Will it
please? Will he put me on his lap and kiss me? Will it save my life?

Women wearing navy threadbare coats in breadlines, shoulder
to shoulder in falling snow. Twenty million widows. Thirty million
widows. And women squatting beside burlap sacks of silver fish the
size of children's fingers in island markets where they speak a bastard Dutch or French. Where they string painted fabrics on ropes
and call them walls, and the edges are determined by wind. Women
in plazas of papayas on afternoons of hillside church bells, alleys of
dirt and no clouds. I considered women in river markets in Asia,
holding white umbrellas and studying fish arranged with their eyes
bulging shocked in the same direction, as if in death they continued
to transmit vital information. And women holding orbs like round
sea-polished stones. They purchase edible roots that resemble fetuses near shops where chickens, shrunken and orange as radiation
burns, hang on hooks in windows.

The woman holds the pear in her palm, evaluating it as one
might an emerald or piece of jade. She is not thinking of her transgressions or regrets. She was not bold enough at the junctures. She
shrugs. She has no affinity for revision. She observes sunlight across
the hard body of the pear. And what of the mysterious stark green

158

avocados softening reluctantly beneath virescent storm clouds in Costa Rica? Will they come to this port next? Last week oranges were stacked against the back windows, their scent went directly through the glass into her arms and breasts.

When she holds an orange in her fingers, afternoon is citrus and stalled. Oranges invent their own science, their own laws. And mangoes with skins embossed as if by a definitive sunset. When she closes her eyes, there is no silence in the dark. In her night she hears the music of remote autumn constellations. Stars talk with their brilliant white as communion veils and lily mouths. Stars with their hunger and infants, negligence and inadequacy. They trade in rumor and gossip.

She is gone. Vanished. A chameleon old woman. I look behind sacks and crates. I ask the man with the scale and apron, "Do you know her name? The old woman with the pear?"

"Why do you ask?" He wants to know, stops making melons into plateaus and looks directly at me.

"She is the most interesting person I have met in France. She has monumental intellect and subtlety. Picasso should kiss her feet." Beyond Paris are forests, bark like cellos, that sheen. And leaves stained auburn like a mother's hair.

"How would you know? She doesn't speak. She barely breathes," the man reveals.

"We spoke," I assure him. "What is her name?"

The man reflects on his possibilities. "Gabrielle." He decides to tell me, then returns to his melons.

The trees are like wild rags in reverse, rising, roots blown loose. They are like celestial aberrations, unanchored, improvising their routes. Currents run between women and trees, insomnia and lightning. Trees waving their stumps like women talking with flags from ships. The earth is a trough, boulevards muted as a dusk mirror. Between illumination and a severed vein is a single camera angle. Did you blink? Was there contamination? Do you have proof?

I stood where boulevards fork. A juncture. A pause. Each avenue was exposed, empty and ruined. My foot bled. I could have stopped breathing. My mouth was useless. I spread my hands wide, trying to suck air through my fingers.

It's a season of incineration. I am home in the Casa Azul. My clothes are wet and I am shivering. "Are you Nurse?" I ask.

Diego drained the air from my room while I was sleeping. He replaced it with ocean water. The pope told him to do it and Diego made a vow. He carried it in himself, without assistants, one bucket at a time.

Silent other. The silver of the tray gleams. The tray with a syringe and a glass vial. A pitcher of iced water. Night obviously. She helps me drink.

"Are you Nurse? Will you bring me Demerol instead?" I tell her where it is.

"Yes, Doña Frida. Do not worry." She makes the hush pantomime with her fingers. "It's very late. Everyone sleeps, even the doctor."

Cautious. I must be cautious with my mouth. I spread my fingers, hold them over my lips. I still have hands. I am trying to breathe through my palms. I must hide my mouth with my pirate stumps. A black baby's fingers stuck in my gums. That's why I can't eat. Baby fingers are too soft and gluey. They don't yet know they need baby saws. They haven't read Kafka or Lorca.

"Is it the same day after the first day? Where is Diego? Where is my birthday?" I begin to cry.

"I am here, Doña Frida," Nurse says. She whispers. "It's very late. You have a vast fever. Everyone sleeps, even the doctor. I have what you want."

"The Demerol?" My eyes are opened now.

Nurse gives me Demerol. I want three. She lets me have three bottles. "Give me, please," I remember to whisper. When Nurse puts the needle in, she finds flesh on my back and thigh. I am more experienced. I put it in veins and make it go directly to my heart. Mainline. Bull's-eye. I set bonfires in my nerves. I still have a vein that hasn't collapsed or broken. It is in my wrist. I slide the second injection in. Then another.

Nurse points to my heart. Does she want to touch me? She is sliding the cotton gown from my shoulders. If I had a back, I would arch it, expose my breasts. My nipples are hard. Nurse has solid fingers, yes. "Suck," I say and she does. "Louder. I want to hear your mouth." We die like we lived, a doctor in Detroit told me. No sudden personality changes. We are what we have been, only less vivid, slower, grayer. "Amuse me," I whisper. Even now. Are we not astonishing?

Then Nurse holds a fresh cotton gown, guides it over my head. "The blood from your cough," she explains. "And the fever."

"You licked me," I say.

"No, Doña Frida," Nurse lies. "You imagine. Here." She fills the syringe with Demerol. She holds her big fingers around my wrist like a tourniquet.

This is not the same day. This is a day of strawberries and raspberries and rivers that leak in. Flood me. Bury me in water and iris and lake. Give me your lips. Kiss me in indigo. I open my mouth with its dark spikes like pilings under a pier. They are night flowers. Amaranth. Jasmine. Swim to me. Surrender to the current.

I sleep. I wake. I am floating on the veranda of the Casa Azul into the harbor of San Francisco. A lattice of bridges growing like lily stalks. Diego comes and goes. Nurse. A new one. A doctor. Silence. Rain. Inverted canals. They have turned Mexico upside down. A punctured ocean. Lilacs and hyacinths fall in. Somewhere, a pear orchard, an inn with fifteen windows facing the sea. A woman in a straw hat carries a basket of peas and strawberries. Her name is Gabrielle. I see her hands. She has stigmata. Rain falls from her palms. "This is how seas are formed," Gabrielle tells me in her child's voice. "From the nailed hands of women who took wrong turns. And from damaged orphans. Abandoned babies. Survivors of trolley car collisions."

"You tell everyone everything." Diego is annoyed. "You're delirious. You're out of order, Frida. What do you want? A press conference?"

Out of order as in a courtroom, where there is punishment? Or out of chronological order? A woman can be punished for this. Men invented these sequences, how to build the Stock Exchange Luncheon Club, cathedrals and roads, airplanes, concentration camps, and machine guns. They play cards and bet on bulls and horses, but they do not believe in chance. How a piano nocturne on a silvery November afternoon just before rain falls is indelible. An eighty-two-year-old French woman named Gabrielle who has official documents, no seaside inn, whispers her intimate regrets in your ear, and your life alters course.

We return from New York, where we were no longer welcome. Diego, a drunken captured animal in the ship cabin that was too small for him. He complains incessantly. "It's like a rat's cage, Frida. Why don't you stay permanently?"

"Stop it. Forget New York, Diego. They were capitalist swine," I remind him, gently. "They're dilettantes of pleasure. They're tourists, not committed."

"It's true, Frida. Hold me." I held him and he wept.

I am older. The lighting and proportions have changed. The seductive pinks of adobe in late afternoon light startle me. The subdued glare of orange tile. A conflagration of jacaranda at the margins. Perimeters of fire. Danger on the patio. A profusion of strange birds and insects.

"You're a spectacle," Diego says, smokes. "I should sell tickets."

"Is it my birthday?" I want to be certain.

"You hemorrhaged through your birthday, my sweet lady of atrocities. You overdosed twice. You coughed up half a lung." Diego is pale, strained.

"What did it look like?" I am interested.

"Like poisonous jellyfish," Diego says. "Matted. Gelatinous"

"Worse than Detroit?" I laugh.

I cough, blood slides from my mouth. Diego's hand trembles. He calls Nurse. He yells. I want to help him. He is so frightened. I will put my arms around him. But I can't move. I only have one leg. I scream. I howl until Nurse gives me morphine.

It is before Paris. It is after Flora's birth and her loss in the marketplace near the airport. Diego and I divorce and remarry. Diego and I have moved into our twin houses as if architecture were a cure. A bridge from the roof terrace connects the two houses. They are not twin and they are not symmetrical. San Angel. How I did not quite move in, find my berth, anchor.

The larger house is for Diego, of course, for his studio, for the monuments he creates to honor himself, and his ambition. The central room is a bus depot crowded with his visitors and whores. Whores from the campo, still stinking of mud and chicken crap and the residues of having sucked off every lieutenant and

Priest within fifty miles for a bus ticket. Women dressed to mimic neon, dragging their red light districts behind them. Women who fucked burros for money. Girls who fucked six brothers when Papa was bored with them. Girls who slept on dirt floors without blankets, with a leash around their necks, and ate from the same bowl as dogs. They were instructed to bark during sodomy and beg for more and to say thank you afterward. Diego found solace in their vulgarity. They were without deception. Sophistication would make them cruel, habitual liars. Now their unadulterated coarseness was an innocence.

And whores from cities. They also came. It was a season of hats with veils and shoes with five-inch heels. They wore tight dresses from Brazil. They wore brazen tiger- and leopard-spotted prints. It was a season when any whore who could spell her name thought she was Eva Perón.

The smaller house was for me and the diminishing details of our domestic life. My attempts to vanish were succeeding. I had already become smaller, less valuable. I was in a metal cast for three years. It was almost impossible to make love. We were mouth to yellow mouth as in a contagion. We were an epidemic. We kissed without teeth. We made ourselves sick. We bit each other. We were laminated with the fingerprints of other lovers. Our infidelities were luminescent. We could see through our skin. We were afraid to be with each other in the dark.

Perhaps it was then that I heard about the affair. Diego and Cristina. We are each in a separate aviary. We are caged, racked by wind and a constant agitation. The jostling at the mirrored seed stand where we try to ring the plastic bell and stay alive another day. I did not need to look in a mirror to paint myself with necklaces of thorns digging into my throat.

"It's a passing amusement," Diego tried. "It's like two of you. Twins. It's entertaining, like incest."

"It's like carnage," my voice ripped out of my mouth.

Diego was silent.

"You bought her two sofas," I yelled.

"I will purchase two sofas for you tomorrow," Diego offered.

"You're an asshole. I'll never fuck you again," I told him. Then I moved out.

I rented an apartment in Mexico City. I opened no windows, had no interest in gardens and verandas. I lived within myself. I hired a car and driver and searched plazas, alleys, boulevards, parks, vegetable and fruit markets for María Elena Campos, the woman with the one pink eye and swollen feet that I had given my daughter, Flora Violetta, to.

It had been in the courtyard of a cathedral near the airport. There had been a market in a plaza, melons and fish and toys, molting saddles and tortillas. The district changed. Banks and stores with refrigerators and radios where there had been cows. Perhaps María Elena had moved back to her pueblo, Córdoba. She might have died from influenza or gotten married. She might work indoors now, embroidering blouses with Aztec symbols in red and green threads. She might stitch yellow daisies on the collars of children's dresses.

Or she might be a platinum-blonde whore with a hat, a net of pink veil, and a matching suit with pearls at her throat. A whore who claimed she was American, from Texas, perhaps. Betty. Her body was fleshy, maggot soft, lips that quiver and whisper lies and say oh baby. Maybe she was here after all. She might be at Diego's studio.

I examined the city by plaza, park, and alley. I had the driver stop. I limped out. Sometimes I needed crutches. I crossed cobblestones and dirt, hobbling, circling the perimeter. Each corner was a juncture, a new trajectory opening like a kaleidoscope.

A man, teeth with gaps where you could see clouds pass. A goat tied with a rope to a tamarind tree. An alley with small men on burros. Women balanced baskets of peppers and lemons on their heads. Bicycles. Pieces of machines. At the foot of a statue of a general on horseback, a woman nursed an infant, dirt and urine from goats and children under her bare feet. A stall where a man sold bags of grain. A man with a rusty scale and an armload of cilantro. Even the ground looked disturbed.

Wires cut the sky. Sisters hunched above a pot almost boiling. A woman on a gray burro that was missing an eye. Alleys encrusted with malicious shadows, a water pump, women in a line with buckets and pails and jars and what had been kerosene jugs. A bed of straw where a boy kneeled, pointing with agitated fingers at the heads of goats and pigs for sale. Washed sheets between wooden and adobe buildings with enclosed courtyards of bougainvillea and cactus, broken radios with their wires showing, rusted pots, old cans, rubber tires, chickens pecking at patterns in dirt passing clouds briefly made.

I spoke with vendors of woolen blankets. I asked the sellers of watermelons and lacquered bowls. I asked children with carved wooden boxes, statues of Montezuma and panthers. I offered dollars to sellers of beads and pineapples, rebozos, horchata. And sellers of straw, silver, cotton, leather, papier-mâché, lead, horns carved from bone. Did they know? Had they seen? Had they heard? Were there rumors? Were there vestiges, a trail like a bird might leave, a scattering of stray seeds? Not me, Señora. I'm not the one. Further in the alley, someone threw a stone.

I fled to New York, where I had many lovers. I collected bodies in my bed. They were like so much sand, debris from a drying ocean. I was anesthetized. They were grit, sharp pebbles. I didn't even count their numbers. New York was a quarry.

Some men ran from my scars and abscesses, my swamp mouth with nubs of charcoal teeth that were falling out. The oddness of my casts. The complexity of making love. The way I wouldn't take off my shoes. I kept a box stuffed with run-from-me articles. Umbrellas, monogrammed scarves, gloves, hats, sunglasses, silk ties, a gun, pipes, car keys, gold cuff links. I called this box my hopeless chest.

In between, I drank tequila and brandy. I drank vodka. I kept a list of doctors I had met at museum and gallery openings, at dinner parties on Fifth Avenue and Park Avenue. They gave me morphine.

"How could you do this to me?" I asked Diego. We were speaking on the telephone. There were time zones between us and official borders. I found this a comfort.

"I did nothing to you. I did it to Cristina," Diego said.

"You made me bad," I accused him.

"You talk like a child," Diego says. "You were bad already."

"I had a capacity for small flirtations. You made me a whore," I remember.

"You said tokens were boring. You said you wanted more. I gave you more. I gave you everything," Diego decides.

"Was it that way with Cristina?" I am angry.

"It's that way with everyone," Diego sighs. "That's the theme. Then the variations."

"You take them by surprise?" I am holding a syringe and a bottle of morphine.

"They take themselves by surprise. The cinema tells them the bad man is sleek and carries a knife," Diego says.

"They don't expect the fat man with the silver-plated pistol?" I tease him.

Diego is thinking, comes to a conclusion. "We are a partnership, Frida."

"The show must go on," I offer.

"It's part of being contemporary," he finally says. I am holding a bathrobe belt in my teeth as a tourniquet. I plunge the needle into my vein, open my mouth, releasing the tourniquet, and citrus, avenues of citrus under lamplight. A plaza of cinnamon. My lungs have forests within. Orchards. Vineyards.

"Basta," Diego yells. "I want you home immediately."

"I don't remember what you look like. I wouldn't even go to your funeral." I hang up.

America or the twin houses in San Angel? That literal geography did not matter. There were only two rules. I must find Flora Violetta. And I must continue my preparations for vanishing.

What did I require? I should be familiar with the languages of opera and also with those of antiquity. Greek and Hebrew. There was an appealing element in Chinese, in the visual spectacle of the script. And Arabic texts which resembled tracks birds leave in sand at the lip of oceans.

For one entire month, I accepted invitations from patrons, went to dinner parties, gallery openings, restaurants. I slept with anyone who asked. When no one asked, I volunteered. I wanted Diego to hear the rumors.

It was summer, I remember the stick of the heat. I considered the scripts that appear only on gold and bronze coins in museum display cases. These cases were opened for me. Curators let me sit alone in cubicles with them. I held the coins in my hands and waited to disappear. Even vanished women need money.

I traced royal faces. I possessed an intricate Braille. I stole two gold princes. The coins were a network of neurons sparking in my skirt pocket. I carried my antiquities into the street, and they were embers, explosives, the final expression of a process that began with flint.

Then it was an American early fall. I went to the country estate of J. P. Morgan. Perhaps it was of John Rockefeller or Henry Ford. The train pushed west into the interior until dusk. An apple orchard ringed the stone house. Apples were turning tawny like the cheeks of fevered infants. Cries of owls and fox. The sweetness of apples was overwhelming, intoxicating. I stumbled without moving. Apples were like lanterns at eye level. My bones felt glazed and inflamed. Raw wind, moonlight defining limbs strung thick with silky yellow bellies. Not apples at all but dead babies ripped from their shells. I knew what this was called. This was C-section farmland.

Later, I opened the window of my room. I knew what they were doing in the forest. They were hanging the stillborns to oak and maple limbs, cauterizing them, stitching them with gut and the razor light that falls from stars. I stood naked as ruins with only my plaster cast and leather shoes. I was barely breathing. I gasped in electric spasms, pushing in air that stung.

I refused dinner, walked uncertainly in the dark, so dark. There was a fenced garden. A trellis with clematis. Rows of corn and tomatoes. The peas and strawberries were ripe. I ate them, forty, fifty, crawling on my knees and snapping them off by moonlight. I promised to return. It was imperative. I forced my eyes wide and remembered the vegetables ripening, the handfuls of peas and strawberries I'd eaten. It had something to do with vanishing. This was more important than coins. Peas and strawberries, I think on the train back to New York City.

Diego telephones in the middle of the night. It is late autumn, a light snow, the first. How little of winter is really white. Insomnia is yellow in all seasons. "I didn't wake you," Diego begins.

"How would you know?" I pour brandy into a glass.

"You don't sleep at night. You're feral. You shoot morphine and arrange your hatreds."

"Is this foreplay?" I have shot three vials of morphine into the vein in the crook of my elbow. I was not asleep.

"Foreplay?" Diego repeats. "You stalk young bodies. You've become a flesh bandit. Everyone knows."

I laugh. I am enjoying this.

"I'm bored with Cristina. Incest is overrated. You must return at once," Diego says.

"Eat shit," I say. "Choke on your feces."

"What will you do without me?" Diego wanted to know.

I poured more brandy. Many vanished women tell fortunes. I could sleep in alleys or courtyards. I could read tarot cards. I could place a board on a straw bale and use it as a table. Instead of flowers, a red scarf in my hair and gold pirate earrings. They would cast ovals across my stylized painted face. People would pay to fish through my eyes for their drowned or consumptive loves. I would sense who had cancer, who was fraudulent, who would die by heart seizure or poison. I would know the truth but lie.

"You will be recognized as insane without me. Without my protection," Diego said. He seemed reasonable, prepared. "You hallucinate. You're a morphine addict. You'll be arrested, Frida. It's a fucking Puritan country up there. They're allergic to pleasure. Even color and rhythm terrify them. And they hate junkies."

"I am careful," I say.

"You inject yourself during dinner parties. You do it on buses and street corners. In prison, there are no doctors. They'll take away your morphine. Your lipsticks. They'll put you in a strait-jacket in Bellevue Hospital. Am I not a better alternative?" He sounded plaintive.

"I'll take my chances," I said.

"Frida, you need me," Diego said, voice soft.

"For what?" I looked at the telephone.

"To save you from yourself. I give your agony focus," Diego said. "I divert you. I'm entertaining."

I hung up. I dragged myself to taxicabs. I went to museums and coin stores. I turned the pages of illuminated medieval manu-scripts. If I stopped, I would be paralyzed. My toes were decaying in my shoes. I slept with my shoes on. I was afraid to see them turning auburn. They were having their own autumn. They would curl and fall.

Alone, without the immensity of Diego, his physical presence and the psychological field he cast, I was acutely aware of my body. I felt my back under the newest cast, splintering. My appendages wanted to surrender. My limbs were trying to escape me. I must stay upright, mobile. I gauged my journey by number of city blocks. I counted trees and signs in windows. In the furrows of alleys, I gave myself morphine.

Days were a sequence of convulsive elations culminating in afternoons lucid and indelible. New York painted my skin as it did its alley walls and subways. I had graffiti on my arms, on the under-sides, in the crook of my elbow. Streets were an act of intimacy and a reprimand. I practiced silence in French. I was uneasy, felt something was grazing at my shoulder.

"Are you still there?" Diego asked. He called in the awkward stutter before dawn. "Have you disappeared yet?"

"Not yet," I admitted.

"Get up and pack," Diego said. "This is becoming bad for business." He asked me to come home, to our twin houses with their bridge in San Angel, and I did. Diego gave my pain counterpoint. He provided a context.

My shoes were fouled from within. I thought of ports in which the cholera dead have been thrown and corpses float brilliant as stars, bloated and rancid, each a lighthouse where a rat would live.

I stayed in my bed in my house that was smaller than Diego's. We were connected by a bridge that was merely symbolic. I rarely crossed it. I was confined to a wheelchair. We are all isolated and exposed, and our connections to one another are filaments.

When I was well, when I could move my fingers and arms, I painted. My easel attached to my wheelchair. I was consumed with my paintings that were not self-portraits, but scientific experiments. They were blueprints and directions. I was using pigments to vanish. Memory is a construct, a series of sketches in constant fluctuation. It is an artifice. I did not look into the mirror but through it. I painted myself as an infant nursing from a golden breast under a sky with stars like tears. I painted cactus like severed hands bleeding. My fruits were carnivores. I painted multiple Fridas. There is a theme and variations. We live our incarnations simultaneously. You learn this in the aviary, if you don't go deaf or mad.

When Diego was gone, when the weather was not too vivid or compelling, when the clouds were tame, I would search for Flora. The driver took me in my wheelchair. I knew each plaza, each cathedral, the ruts, the patches of mud. And the alleys winding behind, into a rubble of stark adobe and stone.

"Where is Flora?" I ask the vendor of green melons. A street of adobe and carved wood slats, holes where there once were windows, crushed grates. Soiled air. Stale candies and piñatas hanging by wires.

"My cousin saw her in Puerto Vallerta. She lives by the ocean. She's married to a fisherman." The melon seller says.

"What kind of fish?" I ask.

"Tuna and marlin." The vendor stares at me. "Also dorado," he adds, after a moment. "The ones that look green when you pull them from deep water."

I laugh, delighted. I pay him. We smile at one another.

A family passes in an oxcart with enormous wheels, sacks of oranges on the bottom. Paper flowers on the top. The ox is white and adorned with bells around the neck, little bells from Oaxaca.

"Have you seen Flora Violetta?" I ask, showing the oxcart driver my money.

The man removes his straw hat, tilts his head in respect, as he would at a funeral. "Flora is in the capital. I told you last month," he says.

175

"What is she doing?" I am suspicious. I am child size in my wheelchair. The palm trees are stiff and flawed, stenciled on a slag sky.

"She is a nurse, Señora. Remember? My sister-in-law's niece saw her in the white uniform. She is respected," the paper-flower vendor says. "She has much authority."

"What kind of nurse?" I demand.

"The kind with the cross of red on her pockets." He smiles. His teeth are fetid.

"What sort of nursing does she do?" I persist. "Does she work with lepers? With the burned?"

"Exactly," he says. "Also with blind children."

This makes me happy. I pay him American dollars.

The alley jogs right into darkness, left into shadow. The cobblestones are broken. I must be careful with my wheelchair. Children squat in patches like pigeons. Women balance clay water jugs on their heads, baskets of dirty clothing, grains, and hot peppers. An alley of young women naked above the waist, washing themselves with soap flakes in a smear of sun, laughing. A boy with a goat. Piles of burlap sacks. Men unconscious, drunk on battered cobblestones. Boards where there were once doors and terraces.

Further, a man in a torn shirt leans against bags of laundry on a platform. He smokes a cigar, spits, sits with his filthy feet showing. He watches me with hard eyes. He sells secrets and contraband. He looks like he just sucked his nine-year-old daughter's breast, stuck two fingers into her vagina, made a circle inside with his fat knuckles bent, and said, "Get used to it."

"What news of Flora Violetta?" I ask. He knows me and that I pay.

"The same. She's an americano's mistress. She's pregnant with another blond son." He offers his back-alley smile. His family has fed themselves by peddling their children and their lies for two generations. It's easier than farming. Still, I pay.

Wheelchair on uneven stones. Push and slide. Push and slide. I am the size of the children, the men sitting, the women squatting, offering warm meats. Chickens. Dogs. A cathedral where stained glass windows turn the sanctuary into a brassy grotto. Pregnant women sleep there when it's hot.

A boy smaller than my wheelchair runs up to me, cigarette butt in his mouth. He holds a bent gray fish in each hand. The fish are curved like bloodied plantains. "Señora. Just for you. Very cheap."

I decide to hit him if he comes closer. I need a shot but where to go? The church? The alley is darkening. Woven red clothing hanging above stones. Wires and balloons. Girls dressed in school uniforms for sale in doorways. Their older sisters wear high heels that accentuate their fine legs. They have thin waists, red mouths, and necks dabbed with jasmine. They are also for sale. On the cobblestones, booklets about Jesus and the army. Pamphlets about saints and not fucking your children or sheep. No burros or chickens, either.

I wheel myself toward the waiting car. I've only managed to search two streets. Then I see the barber. Today he has set up his chair and table behind a cart of roots and lemons. On the ground, an inexplicable pile of seashells, bleached thin as fingernails, circles, ovals, white moons.

The barber has pulled his chair into the shade. His implements are on the table, a mirror, a plastic basin, water, scissors and razors, a bottle of cologne, one squirt only. Men sit in the chair. The barber makes them handsome. He will also trim beards and mustaches. He has skilled hands. He was in the army. He will use his implements for abortions. This is costly. And he sells marijuana. I am a special customer. I buy morphine. It is ready. Two hundred vials wrapped in a paper bag.

"Any word?" I ask. I cannot wheel myself further. The driver starts the car. He will bring the car to me. "Do you hear any rumors?"

The barber is grave. I pay him for his silence.

The driver picks me up, carries me to the car, folds the wheelchair. I lean back. The sky has been rendered absolutely flawless right to the horizon. It is not midnight or cobalt, not turquoise or aqua or any blue with a name that can be spoken. In the end we choose our bruises, I think, and smile. The driver stops in tall palm shadows and I give myself an injection.

My abnormalities become tolerable. I accommodate the toxins, the surgical residues, what I suspect is growing beneath the plaster. I will be in the wheelchair permanently. I will not walk with Flora under a white silk parasol along a river.

We are driving back to the twin houses of San Angel. Behind me, a sunset of balloons above dust, cactus, ferns, two dead gray fish.

The palms. The ripped-apart cobblestones. Sullen dusk and no Flora.

Mutes do not lack the facility for speech. It is simply that they have been taken by surprise. Moss grows on their tongues, as it does along canals. If mutes spoke, rivers would pour from their mouths. They take a vow of silence so they don't drown anyone.

Fierce morning. Bronze and platinum. Diego weeping. Cristina kneeling on the floor, praying. A bouquet of glaring yellow lilies. Yellow. Christ. Were they subconsciously admitting their cowardice?

"Am I dead?" I ask.

"Not yet," Diego says.

"That's good, because I expect more flowers," I say. "And of a better quality. Gardenias and roses. And more ceremony."

Diego nods his enormous head. He's begun to resemble a pre-Colombian stone statue. His face is becoming squat, indio. He blows his nose. Is he disappointed? I am dying as fast as I can.

Cristina rises, gestures to the pathetic lilies, as if I could possibly have missed them, and says, "I love you." She is tremulous.

"We love you," Diego adds.

"What day?" I ask. "Did I miss my birthday?"

"You've slept. It's the sixth day now," Cristina says.

"Am I dying?" I want to know.

"Yes," Diego says. He is miserable.

Silence. Songbirds, perhaps tanagers. Sky darkening so soon. It will rain again.

"But I'm not finished," I reveal. What of my personal records, my accounts receivable?

"Frida, you are most definitely finished," Diego says. "You've died three times. Doctors barely brought you back. You've coughed out your lungs like diseased fish. You bleed from the nose and ears. Your fever is past measurement."

Diego is smoking. He gives me a cigarette, pours tequila in a glass. Cristina is also drinking, biting her lip, the center is pulpy like ruined fruit. Cristina taps my glass with hers. We smile and toast.

"I had a priest bodily removed, carried out," Diego says, laughs. "There's a line to give you last rites."

"Don't let them." I look directly at him.

"That goes without saying," Diego says. " Do you want burial?"

"As opposed to being thrown in the street and eaten by wild dogs?" I say. I want my breakfast. It comes in a clear glass vial. I get four.

"There's cremation," Diego offers.

I hadn't considered this erasure into ash. To remember is to delude the self. To keep artifacts is to risk blindness. To disappear in flame has style. I would be extinct. "Yes," I tell Diego. "I want to be burned."

"It's done," Diego says.

On the veranda, the brutal sun is retreating. Morning turns

damp from moss and berries and promises that broke like young women's legs, all the marrow leaking out. I called my lies tributaries. I thought myself an ocean.

"We kissed with our teeth and it wasn't enough," I say.

"It was more than enough," Diego disagrees.

"I lived at a shocking altitude," I realize.

"You shocked everyone," Diego admits.

"I shocked myself. Am I still alive?" I ask.

"Yes," Cristina says. She has tears on her cheeks. Her eyes are rubbed raw.

"You saw your face in a mirror where there was no mirror," Diego observes, considers something, glances at his watch, bends, and kisses my forehead. He prepares to leave.

"Wait," I cry. Diego waits.

"Did I go to the campo with Nelson Rockefeller? A house surrounded by apple trees? Ripening and sweet?" I almost remember. Leaves like swaying chiffon. The half-naked maples, martyrs smelling of pumpkin and tea rose. Reds insistent and inflamed, yellows so fevered the ground blistered and stung. I could see in the dark. I knew where to walk.

"You went everywhere with everyone," Diego decides. "Tell Cristina what she wants before you die." Then he has left the room, my bedroom in the Casa Azul where it will soon rain.

Cristina wants to know what happens next, after this self-aware interlude. She thinks hell is like Cuba in August. The church penetrated her and induced a delusion of hierarchies and increments of punishment. She believes the dead must pack sun-tan lotion.

I do not recognize Nurse. I ask what has happened.

"You scared the other one away," Cristina says. "Now the doctor says you can have Demerol whenever you want."

"In my veins?" I feel cheerful.

"In your eyes. In your nipples. It's fiesta time," Cristina says. Bitter. Bitter, bitter little buttercup.

The vein in my wrist is collapsing. I have to slap it repeatedly. Cristina's fingers make a tourniquet, tight and release. Ah, glassy kisses with a tongue down a throat. It doesn't matter if I have fluid in my lungs. Haven't I been a vessel? A water woman?

"Please, sister," Cristina, bleary-eyed, lips bitten. Fingers chewed by rosary. Knee blisters. She thinks this is suffering.

"A country road, winding slow through low mountains. Green forests. A harbor with a lighthouse. The stranger approaches a stone house surrounded by apple trees. They are ripening." I pause, pour tequila.

"This is Jesus," my sister divines.

"His name is Frank." I am amusing myself. "Sunset comes like a ravishment. Then a flock of burgundy jungle birds flies above the balcony where he sits naked in a rented room."

Cristina takes a breath. "What is he doing?"

"He is watching the sunset while he plays guitar." I can see this, yes.

"And that is all?" Cristina stares at me.

"Is it not enough? Yes. That is all."

Cristina takes my hand. I am an oracle now. My flesh blesses. She places her lips on my fingers and kisses them.

The affair with Trotsky was foolish and poignant in all the wrong ways. I had no interest in politics. Men held the ideas, formed strategies. Women were supposed to sit silently supportive while the men smoked cigars and argued.

The women served coffee. The men composed tracts and dictated them. The women typed. They ran duplicating machines, breathing in tainted magenta fumes. The machines broke constantly. I was nauseous and dizzy. I had headaches. I put my head on a box of leaflets exhorting the peasants to action and fell asleep.

"It's ludicrous," I informed Diego.

"I know. But I beg you. Tell no one," Diego said, glancing behind his shoulder as if expecting assassins, secret police.

Diego was president of the Communist Party of Mexico. I was outraged when he accepted the position. "You'll have to go to all the meetings," I realized. Diego shrugged. He would wear his Stetson hat and twirl his silver pistol to cheer himself up.

I refused to attend Communist Party meetings on aesthetic grounds. The hard metal portable chairs. The grotesque lighting, how it accentuated skin and grayed it. The men's beards were dirty.

Their eyeglasses greasy with fingerprints and food. Everyone looked like they lived in a basement.

Trotsky, in exile, came to see us. We were part of the tour. After the airport, the museum with Aztec and Mayan artifacts and sundials, it was lunch with the Riveras. Frida and Diego, the new ruins. You can't miss them. She's a bolted-together cripple who talks like a stevedore. He's the size of a boat. It's always cocktail hour at their place. The house is a brothel. Their life is theater. There's a line. Get a ticket.

Everyone came. Soccer legends and cinema directors. Inventors and art historians. Anthropologists and curators. An Arabian princess who was having an affair with a leper. Gangsters with molls who wanted to tango. Artists and exiles. Ambitious whores. Poets and smugglers. Brothers of people we didn't even remember.

Diego met Trotsky's ship. He was still president of the Communist Party. He hadn't fired himself yet. Leon reminded me of a mathematics professor at a university for the mediocre. He was pinched and chalky. He talked constantly, using his hands for further emphasis, repeating his sentences as if his brilliance required immediate duplication. He lacked style. Even Diego was disappointed.

I loathed his wife, Natalia. She had a round Slavic face and too much forehead. She could have been a bourgeois matron in Detroit, perhaps, obsessively showing photographs of sons who were all medical doctors. But she was too nervous, lacked authority. She was plump, shaky, flatfooted. She ate as if her family had been starving for centuries. She was agitated, haphazard, completely displaced. She did not brush her long black hair but rather tied a scarf around her scalp instead. She didn't wear perfume or lipstick. Her face was weathered raw like a farmer's. She missed nothing and watched the events around her with eyes brilliant and confrontational.

Diego arranged for them to stay at the Casa Azul. He thought it would make headlines and it did. Trotsky seized me with passion and made love to me as soon as we were alone. First he performed, reciting political passages from arcane philosophers while I sat in a chair. Was I supposed to clap? I shrugged and clapped. He recited stanzas of poetry. Then he leapt at me, dragged me onto the floor, spread my legs and paused. He seemed confused and exhausted. He would have preferred to keep talking.

We made love in this fashion, with dramatic recitation, several times. Leon confessed that he was frightened. My ridges of scar terrified him. He said I looked like I had been interrogated repeatedly by the secret police. I gave him marijuana to smoke and he took three short puffs and trembled with fear. He turned bleached and filmy. He asked for a blanket and pulled it over his face.

Natalia made an appointment to visit me for tea. Tea again. I remembered Chinatown in San Francisco. I could have stayed with Jane, moved into her studio, and had an entire other life. Perhaps I could have crossed the bridge, settled in a northern county, in a redwood house on a hill, had teas and spices in graceful jars labeled with calligraphy. Rain would have been an enticing tapping, like an invisible infant's feet.

Natalia studied me with eyes that sparked. "What a getup," she finally said. "Does he force you to wear that crap?"

"I'm used to it. And I have no tea. Only coffee," I informed her.

"I figured. I've brought the tea," she said. She unwrapped leaves resembling beard stubble. Her fingers were huge and assured. She could have been a farmwife. She was compact, sturdy, large-boned, strong. Her cheeks were chafed. She didn't use oils or powders. Now she was somber, controlled. She was prepared to negotiate.

Natalia had a smart leather suitcase leaning against her leg. The buckles were shiny. They might have been gold. The case was new. Natalia placed it on the kitchen table where there was no tea. There was also no coffee. I thought her tea appointment merely a formality. I didn't expect to provide refreshments.

"Leon is nothing to you," Natalia began. "But he is my world. What can I give you to leave him alone?"

"What do you have?" I was curious.

She opened the case. There were statues wrapped in leather pouches and the cloth used for storing silver. Natalia unwrapped them, one slow layer at a time. It was a striptease and I was aroused. I thought they were statues wearing corsets, fertility figures that had been in streetcar accidents and were now encased with casts around their backs. They had neat rows of stitches in scar tissue. The poor things couldn't breathe. Someone should rescue them. Perhaps that is why she had brought them to me.

Finally, the last tissue paper was removed. It was a crystal goblet, not a statue. I understood the craftsmanship without touching it. I sensed its resonance, its value. I looked from the glass to Natalia's field-worker fingers.

"They belonged to the czar," Natalia said. "It's all I have."

"How many are there?" I felt we were playing poker. I drank rum with chunks of pineapple. I was celebratory.

"Eight," Natalia revealed, with grim finality. It was obvious she did not know how to play poker. There was nothing frivolous about her. The Russians were relentlessly serious. And she had shown me her hand. She looked into my snake and monkey face. Bourgeois love and love of possession merged within her. It made her fearless. I liked that. So I agreed.

"You will cease the affair immediately and permanently?" She wanted clarification. Did she want this in writing?

I pretended interest in the goblet. "I give you my word." We shook hands, like men in an American western movie.

"We are finished?" Natalia was prepared to leave.

"I want to shampoo your hair," I said, leading her to the kitchen sink.

I found lotions and towels and hairbrushes in my bedroom. I gave myself a shot of morphine. I was struck by the clarity of the morning, its excellent composition and light. Natalia stood at the sink. I unbuttoned her blouse. I unknotted her scarf, brushed her wiry hair. I anointed her neck with jasmine.

"Now me," I told her.

Natalia washed me as if I were an animal, a sheep or goat, perhaps. Her strong fingers on my scalp, rubbing insistently, thoroughly. She let my wet hair run between her fingers. Her astonishment when we kissed. How bold she became, holding me later on her naked lap, braiding my hair while I sucked her nipple.

I have the goblets still. Soon after, Leon was dead. He was axed through the head and police questioned me. They took me to an interrogation room. Did I bash his skull in half? "I barely knew him," I defended myself. "It sounds like something Diego might do. He loves bold statements. I prefer a slow death. Decay. Organ failure. Poison."

The police drove me home, called me Señora. They did not return.

Diego loved the drama and the goblets. He said I had a knack for deal making. It was in my Jewish blood. It is a gift some women are born with. The police had questioned Diego for two days and a night. He was hungry. We ate in a French restaurant. Later, Diego made a collection of newspaper articles about Trotsky and he saved them for years. I have no idea what happened to Natalia.

I was sick. I was not sick. Fevers. Nausea. Rancid gauze bandages. I drank to disguise the stink in my mouth. I had pills for energy, tranquilization, and sleep. I had tinctures for pain, but only morphine helped. The pharmacies could be generous to a woman in a wheelchair with envelopes of money.

I had moved back to the Casa Azul. I lived in my childhood canopied bed. I had shelves built at eye level to further enclose me, shelves with jars of perfumes and medicines, dolls and bells, idols in wood and stone, boxes for jewelry. People sent me sand from

African beaches, from China and Tahiti, and I saved this. I held my life in my fingers. Diego could be where he chose.

I painted with an easel attached to my bed. My fingers had their own intentions. I could not leave the canvas alone. I crawled to it, slid to it by inches on my belly. I marked my years by gallery exhibitions, hospitals, cities, and surgeries. I traded Trotsky for eight goblets and a shampoo. Later, there was the woman in Paris with the pear, Gabrielle, who had tried and failed to vanish. When I could bear to sit, the driver took me in my wheelchair, and I searched for Flora.

Diego and I divorced. We remarried in San Francisco, a year later, on December 8, 1940. It was my idea, to marry again in the city where our first marriage had so flagrantly failed. It was like returning to the scene of the crime. The city where Diego painted capitalist shrines and I conceived our child, the misplaced Flora. She was not abandoned or dead. She was simply missing. I calculated her age. She was nine.

I searched for Flora in San Francisco. I walked with crutches. I rode cable cars and looked down into alleys for a girl with hair like coffee beans, a girl with braids, perhaps. Once I went to an astrologer to determine the best days for finding missing objects. He said I should look in my hatbox and ask the patroness of wronged virgins to help me. And Saint Zita, patroness of lost keys. In desperation, I limped down to the ships. I called upon any deity in port that day to aid me. Nothing.

Then a long hospital stay, eleven months, a tile-cool gray blank. My paintings were selected for the Golden Gate International

Exhibition, but I was in the hospital. Then we went to New York where the painting of Diego ripping out my two hearts was shown.

"Now everybody knows," Diego mused. "We'll lose our mystery."

"But they knew already," I pointed out.

Wasn't that part of our charm and sales appeal? How our marriage was an architecture of carnage? How the world randomly sentenced me to an unspeakable half-life? How we were a continuous scandal? Then my father died and we returned to Mexico.

Did they amputate then, or later? Was it six months or twelve months in another cast, in another hospital? Was it two surgeries or twelve? When they sawed off my leg, it was a revelation. I discovered a further dimension. The violation was an astonishment. I heard birds and incantations in the hospital corridors. The aviary has forests on its floors. I realized amputation is the juncture of purity and intelligence. It's where the river stops. It's where the river strips.

Then we were home and it was a season of gangsters. Men who carried real guns, bought and sold weapons, canvases, and articles removed from tombs. They dug tunnels, they sifted bones. They spoke five and six languages and had dinners with ambassadors. They gave blue fox and sable coats to their women, who were predators, sharp nailed with thin cruel necks. They could survive the rainforest night and not go hungry.

Diego was not the only man who carried a gun and thought himself international. It was the new style. They called themselves businessmen, claimed to be in import and export, would barter, and I liked this. I imagined Mexico returning to a tribal configuration. This was better than Communism and required no duplicating of pamphlets. I entertained apocalyptic visions of the collapse of transportation and systems of communication.

There would be a return to living in caves, which I would paint. Lore would be chanted, passed mouth to mouth. Trade would be seashells and stones, spices, plants that induce languor and hallucination. I would find Flora and at last and finally, I would be home.

The bodies were meant to be temporary, kindling for the canvas that demanded constant illumination. I loved quickly and indiscriminately, anonymously, seeking some inspired new avenue of impulse I could paint. I might have picked my lovers by lottery. All that remains of these chaotic years are my paintings, which are not self-portraits. They are imprints of a human woman peeling off her flesh and revealing that which is most vulnerable and resistant to definition.

Diego began to build Anahuacalli, his private museum. That is how he measured himself, that is the scale in which he felt comfortable. My home was my canopied bed in Casa Azul. Between operations, between love affairs and dramas, heartbreak and revelation, both Diego's and mine, there were paintings.

I was carried into galleries on a stretcher. Crowds parted, as they do for survivors of natural disasters. Eventually, I was the exhibition. There were my paintings and there was Frida in her Tehauna costume, lipsticked, rouged, just as expected, as demanded. I wore necklaces of silver cars, guns, and hearts. I wore earrings in the form of two hands that Picasso had given me, the two hands he wanted to hurt me with.

"That was much later," Diego says. Nurse is with him. The new one.

"What am I forgetting?" I ask.

"The war," Diego reminds me.

My arm floats, a translucent wing. I am engraved with the intricacy of July buttterflies. I move to narcotics like a plant to sun. This is a sophisticated photosynthesis. I take drugs in and a transformation occurs. I open my swamp mouth and irises come out, moths with wings like the geometric stained glass windows of European cathedrals.

Between exhibitions and parties, hotels and ambulances, there were rumors of brutality in Europe. The Germans again. Jews beaten in their shops. Books thrown into boulevards and burned. Jews were leaving. We met them at galleries. They had taken their paintings. They had cut them from their frames with razor blades and carried them in their suitcases from Berlin and Prague. They were leaving Vienna. There was a lull and then panic.

I was the horizontal woman with so many versions of myself, like so many copper coins. I was a woman carried on a litter like a trophy that breathes. I was a peninsula. In my harbors, rivers concluded themselves, carrying chrysanthemums, urine, the butter and grease from cremations. Women squatted washing cotton. Children drank the port water and discovered they could recite the incarnations of gray like a litany in nine languages.

In hotels, out satin-draped windows, boulevards and rivers were lamplit and jaundiced. My body was dissembling itself. I lost more teeth as I slept. I mashed my food and ate slowly with a child's spoon. My back was a fabric stained by rain and abuse, terror and obsessional extravagance. My back was something you wouldn't want to look at, didn't want to find in an attic after Uncle died. That is why we stumble on the stairs as we climb. It isn't our balance that we lose, but rather our emotional composure. We suspect that our lovers are serial killers. And Uncle. We shudder. We are all capable of everything.

A hotel suite. Diego pouring brandy for men offering commissions. Diego is talking about bombs and museum collections in his terrible fractured English. I cannot help him negotiate. That night, I could not wear any clothing. Even pure cotton made me scream. Lamplight was a lash on my skin. Outside was another city in fall. The blaze of the maples was the least of it.

Whispers about death camps. I thought, I am a portable death camp. I am avant-garde. I have been dying since I was seventeen. They should make a lamp from my back. The scars would provide a unique design.

Solitary autumn. Another hotel. A park below, pale, ashen. Talk of extermination. A glare like a kind of interrogation light came directly out of the landscape. Governments had new procedures for men who hadn't slept in eleven days. Then the forced voluntary confession. The gas chambers for Jews. And those who didn't make love as prescribed. Asymmetry was treasonous. They melted one-legged women into soap. Railroad cattle cars, slatted, cold, carrying the starved, coughing in a Polish winter. International gangsters grabbed their wedding rings, their Monets, the gold teeth pried from their mouths.

Horizontal, corseted, my wounds worsening under fresh plaster. I kept my toes from falling off by taping them with bandages and applying painter's glue. I refused to remove my shoes. I left damp marks in carpets and polished hallways.

Morning. It was not 7 A.M., but the hour of straw and willows. It was not 8 A.M., but the hour of women on patios, hanging shirts to dry on ropes strung between wood slats. In alleys leading to the city, squash and corn and cilantro came in oxcarts from the campo. Then pimps with their sleeping whores. Chickens. Boys on their way to the army or prison. A woman with earrings like two hands that want to strangle. The woman with crutches and a mouth where stumps loiter. The one with the American money looking for her daughter.

I did not consider my condition a limitation. Mornings are an assemblage of evasions. Women in constant pain know this. The recently widowed or miscarried. Women with breast cancer. Women with unfaithful husbands. Women in railway cars suspecting they are being sent to concentration camps, wondering if they should toss their infants to the peasants in cabbage fields who pause, lean on hoes, watch the train. They might take a baby found in a field, a free baby who could later do farmwork. Is that not a more plausible alternative?

Stalled day. Who decrees the quality of light in the arroyo? Who decides which generals become bronzed statues in parks?

Who carries the bundles of wood on their backs? Who orders a waltz rather than a tango? Who patrols the borders? Who defines the properties? Why trust anyone?

"These aren't paintings," Diego shouted, intoxicated on tequila, opium, and cocaine. He had stacked my canvases on the floor. He had a jar of gasoline and a bale of straw. He clapped his hands together and said, "Bonfire time."

"You'll have to burn me." I was suddenly sober. I would crawl across tile, manipulate my body, contort, and protect them. He would have to burn me first.

"These are not paintings. This is not art. It's public debauchery," Diego said. "This is a striptease in front of the world."

Diego cried. Perhaps he broke a chair or a vase or a serving dish with fish etched into the glaze. Then he fell asleep.

The fool. The paintings were not of me. They weren't a striptease but a dissection. Autopsies of the still breathing. It must have been after my exhibition in Paris. I learned every street is a segment of autumn. Every boulevard is an atrocity of lamplight and lindens. In every glass bracelet is the face of your grandmother. If she spoke, she would tell you lies.

Diego. Who knows what barked in his night? What howled in what mesa of nightmare? Perhaps it was the war that made us reconsider. We remarried, understanding we would live apart, permanently. Diego resided in the museum he was building for himself, with his antiquities, his statues, his increasingly expensive relics. He was trying to contrive a method of remaining on this plane indefinitely. I was practicing vanishing. We closed our flesh to each other. Our bodies were a mutual contagion. We had lost our immunity to one another.

"I made you laugh, Chiquita," Diego complains. And voice softer, "You don't tell that story. I accommodated. I amused. We were partners."

I consider Diego singing, rattling a tambourine in one hospital or another. They were stage sets for him. He understood his part. The devoted husband playing at being the buffoon, the fool, the comedic relief, who periodically glances at his watch.

It's easy to tap the tambourine for bedridden women when you know the night will end. Recess and you are released. No more rosaries. No more algebra. It's the bell on a ship, a suggestion, then night opens. It virtually beckons. You can walk or take a cab. You and a woman who knows there are epics in her cheekbones.

I was a failed collage, face to the ceiling. I was given anesthetic. Even then autumn asserted itself. Stands of oak formed across the walls, inverted forests were born above my head. Low branches grazed my hair. Monkeys built nests in vines. I defiled rooms with my jungles. I was fierce and devious. They could not sterilize my thoughts. They wanted me sedated, in a half-sleep. It took a pharmacy to subdue me.

But they could not remove my inspired aberrations. I saw Frida's spine with its twelve barely fused vertebrae. I painted the nails in her flesh. I examined and calculated. Sixty-seven nails impaled her, nails such as a carpenter has. This is neither dream nor metaphor. I painted her bare legs spread in the act of giving birth, vagina like a man's shaved face, peppery stubble. This was called an obscenity. I painted Frida with antlers and arrows in her doe body. She was wildly alert, as if she had been injecting adrenaline, yet still knew to run toward the trees.

The painter and her subject merged. I was a saboteur. I practiced voodoo. I was pagan. I worshipped revolution. I consorted with skeletons and severed body parts. I was nude in many capitals. I committed treason against the makers of the laws, the boundaries, the shapes, the names, the calibrations.

But this is trivial in comparison to my real crime. I gave my infant daughter to a stranger from Córdoba who was selling blankets near the airport. María Elena Campos. A squat woman with rags on her swollen feet, a bell-necklaced burro, and an eye infection. A woman with drowned sons. She smelled of fish and peppers and the salt at the bottom of burlap sacks. I have been searching for her ever since. And my daughter, Flora. I imagine I am holding her. I close my eyes and breathe in winter flannel, cedar, and antique lace kept wrapped in drawers scented with cloves. She is a winter daughter. They have exceptional love for their mothers. They are sometimes nuns or nurses. They have a gift for the sick. Such daughters often elect to stay with their mothers. They read each other adventure stories and poetry. They play duets, piano and flute. They make applesauce in autumn.

One peels apples, the other mashes them in a simmering pot. Flora Violetta. Have you seen her? Can you call her now? Are visiting hours over?

Diego was building Anahuacalli, an appropriate monument befitting a man who is convinced that his murals will be intact for thousands of years. I was confined to my bed with its canopy and mirror, with my special painting easel, with my headboard where I had glued on photographs of Marx and Freud, Einstein and Kafka. I had my trinkets, carvings of warriors and animals. My souvenirs. Children's toys, statues and pottery, boxes of costume jewelry, the innumerable seed and tin amulets I was famous for. My trademarks.

I was imprisoned in my bed. I was confined with Frida. I had only what I could reach with my hands. And sometimes, between ladies of the cinema and heiresses, ladies of inexplicable commonness, ladies who were manicurists or dress-store clerks, Diego had a sense that he had strayed too far. What if he was, in fact, accountable? Then he rushed to my bedside, with bouquets and chocolates, stuffed rabbits, papier-mâché dolls, baskets of melons with balloons large as his head tied onto the handles. Diego smuggled bottles of tequila into the hospital. He would arrive breathless, as if he had been running. Then he would dance like a circus bear at the side of my sickbed. Diego in the last of our theater sets.

What is the circus? A trained horse who counts to five? A lion who dares the fire hoop? The sequin-studded beauty on the high trapeze? She can count sixteen blood relatives who have died doing this sort of work. It runs in the family like hemophilia. Then the audience with their peanuts and savage infantile longing to see her splinter.

Diego and I had perfected a certain choreography. We were Fred Astaire and Ginger Rogers, and we didn't even have to dance. We were Diego, the enormous, and Frida, the publicly mutilated cripple, a couple notorious for their suffering, and infidelities, and adventurous politics. It was a family business. We would take our clothes off for you. You could take us home. Buy a canvas. Buy two.

I howled and tried to put my toes back onto my feet. They were spilling from my shoes and onto the tile hospital floor like stiff worms. I grabbed them, stuck them into the green hollows where they had been, trying to demonstrate that they'd snap back in. Then they amputated my leg. It was the same sort of saw you would use on a farm for a horse or a tree. It was after the final cast. It was after the war. Diego and I recognized that art had its limits, and as a united enterprise, we could pay the high expenses. Our entourage, the doctors and nurses and gallery owners, the camp followers and collectors, the assorted whores and magazine writers, photographers, the exiles waiting for an ax, the wives who shampoo you with confident hands. You are merely another animal, not so different from a foal or lamb.

After the war, after the death camps, after the lampshades made from women's skin, and the melted-down flesh of children used for soap, art stopped. After Hiroshima, after the atom bomb dropped on the sleeping city, the concept of permanence and beauty changed course like a river in a cataclysm.

Cynicism is possible, as long as you still possess a shy and unmolested innocence. You must believe in continuity and transcendence. Without this awe, you might as well paint motion picture sets or the tents of circuses. After the war, the easel was obsolete, like Communism, capitalism, anarchism, all of it. We were barbarians. We constructed objects of entertainment from the skin of children. We released bombs abnormally dense with disturbed atoms, burning nails and worms of manic particles onto sleeping families. Flesh slipped from their bones and hung in the radiated air like luminescent spider webs. They bled from their eyes and lost their minds. They were gutted. The air betrayed them. Blindness was common. They stumbled to rivers, searching for water, but there were too many bodies. You could walk across rivers. And the waters were burning.

I kept painting. Breton, the supreme French idiot, had called me a surrealist. I had said then, not at all. I am painting reality. This is not a dream, my friend. The woman impaled with sixty-seven nails is not a hallucination. The woman with the crenellated column that should be a spine, the woman with her heart ripped out, resting on her blouse like a breathing corsage, is not an invention of the imagination, an exaggeration, or a product of fever. I know this woman.

"She is you," André said. "If not metaphor and dream, this is a visual report of your life. A journal done in paint."

"That would be vulgar," I told him, trying to stay awake. "I know this woman. But we are separate."

"Then that is the dream," André said.

"You are playing a rich man's parlor game. You offend me," I yelled, slammed his door.

After the war, it was obvious that it was I, Frida, who painted recognizable events. Diego was the surrealist, with his slow sun-bloated women, bovine with their corn stalks, their ridiculous lilies, and their enormous static harvests. Diego did not include radium in his palette. He did not acknowledge poisons in the rivers, flowing into vines, into breasts that give tainted milk. According to Diego, Mexico is a region without contamination. I said nothing. Diego painted women embracing sunflowers as if the earth naturally absolved them and would continue to do so. It was Diego who painted dreams.

I was in my child's canopy bed, with my special table, dealing out tarot cards. I evaluated the faces of archetype, so few the types, really. The juggler. The joker. The woman on fire. The virgin in the collapsing tower. The messenger. The clairvoyant. The advisor to the prince.

This century required an updated deck. What of the woman who painted herself with a spinal column you could see through like an unfinished tenement, an abandoned building in a bankrupt province? Where was the woman with swollen feet, one pink eye, and drowned sons? Where was the morphine addict who couldn't use the veins in her legs because they were sawed off?

The new cards would show an old woman, out of focus, partially vanished in an autumn park in Paris. Then a death camp. An atom bomb. A syringe. A doctor with a serrated saw. An exiled revolutionary who talked too much and had an ax implanted in his head. And a card for the serial killer. Where was the card of the lost infant? The infant daughter left near an airport, neatly placed in the center of a monogrammed handkerchief? What of the card showing a girl without official documents, abandoned by circumstance?

I practiced disappearing. Once I vanished, I would expand beyond the invisible bars of my bed and travel undetected. I could enter rooms, watch couples make love, take their money. I was beginning to possess powers. I did not need books to acquire knowledge. It came to me through another process entirely, a separate channel, unabashedly tactile. I was engaged in reconnaissance, surveying the mountain ranges and deserts, the plazas and seasides, where I might go after I disappeared. You might say I was building for my future.

At dusk I repeated the names of the remarkable dead. Karl Marx. Joan of Arc. Oscar Wilde. Garcia Lorca. Anne Frank. I said their names out loud and my bedroom in the Casa Azul thickened with invisible origami. Accidental utterances can become manifest. That is the origin of prayer and incantation. These are the unexpected shrines and why we trip for no reason. They hang like strands of ivy or party decorations along our walls. No one can see them but other disappeared women.

Legions of women have successfully vanished. It is possible I can find them. Perhaps there are concealed subterranean networks. A vanished woman might know Flora. She might be protecting her, teaching her to play the piano and dance ballet. What if the martyrs are not really dead, but rather vanished, removed from the ordinary plane. Perhaps the crypts are empty. Not grave robbers but women erasing their points of exit. They take their gold with them.

"Heaven is an alias and a false address," I tell Diego.

"You are almost completely incoherent," Diego replies.

He is carrying something. Has he brought me a plate of watermelon? What is he holding? Is it a letter? Has he brought me rare flowers with leaves shaped like stars? Are those more fragments of my coughed-up lungs? They are flame red because Diego had them cooked.

Diego taunts me. "What month is it?" He asks. "What year?"

I remember 1950. I was to have another operation. They said it would reduce my pain, an improved surgical technique. So I had bone grafts. It was a travesty. Everything went wrong. They locked me in special plaster. There was no way to paint. I developed seven sequential infections. A tawdry green fungus swept up my legs. Something from the jungle, singular and lethal, crept in. I spent nine months in the hospital.

More of Diego, the dancing bear. It was squalid. Once he sent me a Huichol Indian in formal ceremonial dress to pose for me. I couldn't even hold charcoal in my fingers. The nerves had clamped my hands into fists. That was the hospital where my orthopedic corset was cut from my body with scalpels and knives and the truth underneath was revealed. More fungus, but paler, not as agitated. My back was increments of jade. That's when they said I smelled like a decaying dog, a carcass from war. That's when they injected me with three bottles of Demerol to cut off my shoes. My toes fell off like ten starved rats jumping ship. I had glued and bandaged them onto my feet and now they dropped off like singed petals. The big toes first. Smaller toes spilled from my shoes.

Diego howled. He took out his silver pistol, aimed it at his temple, then the head of the doctor. "I will kill someone," Diego announced.

"Wait," the doctor said, using his hands for emphasis. "This didn't just happen. You must understand. This has taken years."

"She stuffed the dead toes back in? Every day, gluing, concealing?" Diego stared at the door.

"Smell me," I said to Diego then.

He held his forehead in his hands. He slumped into himself. He hid his eyes. He refused to touch me. He said, "I cannot."

"Do it," I commanded. "Do it as a good Communist. As an artist. A Jew. A man. This is modern, Diego. This is international."

Diego wept. He left the room crying. Later, he sent me the Huichol in ceremonial robes and wide hat with bells and seashells on it. The Huichol sang softly, staring down at the floor, embarrassed. Then he danced, a succession of listless hops. It was monstrous. Was this supposed to be entertaining?

"You're a coward," I screamed at Diego. The dancing bear had recently been drinking tequila.

"I know," Diego admitted. He hung his head. "It is my great shortcoming."

"It's but one and minor, really," I replied. "On your list of defects, it wouldn't make the top twenty. And take the poor Indian away. He seems traumatized."

The Huichol was young, perhaps thirty. He trembled from cold or emotional turbulence. Perhaps he felt laminated by the harsh glare of the hospital light. People were moaning in adjacent rooms, dying and having limbs removed. The Huichol had a shy smile. He did not want to dance and sing here.

"What can I bring you?" Diego asked. "Tell me. Anything. Don't consider cost."

"Bring me a leg," I said. "Bring me toes."

Diego produced his bloated circus bear expression, his look of confusion, of the big man humbled by circumstance. This is a mask he learned from the cinema. When I was young, he did not possess this expression.

Oh, Diego. So tactless and ignorant. He knew nothing of our secret daughter, Flora, conceived in San Francisco and birthed badly in Detroit, when Diego thought his murals would survive for centuries. That was why I had to rebirth my daughter in Mexico. She slid from my gutted womb in the garden. I wrapped her in leaves. She fit in my palm. I hid her in a cigarette package in my purse. Then I lost her, misplaced her.

Diego, the dancing bear with the common-man humbled stare. He pushed my wheelchair down the sticky hospital corridor, through the stark generic light. We were too exhausted and stupefied to even insult one another.

Then I was back in my four-poster bed. I painted. I thought about vanishing. I realized that the vanished have extrasensory perception and do not sunburn. They know what stocks to buy and when to sell. It's like learning how to decipher dreams or the hieroglyphics on jungle tombs. They simply have the key to the symbology.

Once I vanished, I would have unusual abilities. Then I could find Flora. I could intuit the procedure. You stand in front of a mirror. You repeat the name of the one you have lost in nine languages. You hold an ordinary city map and bland indigenous flowers in your hand. You must be stealthy, not startle, blend in. The city where the missing one is turns fire red on your map. It falls from your burnt fingers. A bouquet of orchids form at your feet, if you have feet. Then you know exactly where to go.

There are oracles. There are fortune-tellers. Legion are the charlatans, but mixed within are the possessors of indisputable knowledge. Some women look in crystal balls and see the next century. That is why such professions persist. These are the traditional occupations of vanished women. The gypsy wardrobe is optional. I am certain of this. In my next life, no pamphlet duplications, no mimeographing, and no extravagantly exotic costumes. I want to wear trousers and sweaters like Katherine Hepburn. I want short hair, easy to wash and dry and nothing in it, not a single petal or stem, not even wind.

Demerol. It was the holy water for atheists. I was completely converted. It was the mechanism for finding ports of entry. It was the way to count the sails in all the Sunday harbors. I could stay flat on my back with the perpetual wounds I would be buried with and float through centuries. This is what Cleopatra did on her barge. The Nile was incidental to the process.

"You are completely out of order," Diego is saying.

He is wrong. I can remember 1953. Flora is twenty-two years old. I am having my first one-person exhibition in Mexico. The only good woman artist is a dead woman artist, but I am to be an exception. But just barely. They have changed the date of the exhibit, made it six months earlier. That's how close to death I am. But, finally, I am lucky. I, Diego's parrot and monkey woman, the minor painter with the foul mouth and taste for the forbidden, will live to see my paintings exhibited at the Galería del Arte Contemporáneo.

I arrive by ambulance. I am escorted by motorcycle police like a visiting president. I am transported with my face to the sky, to the ceiling. I do not yet know that Frida is the exhibit. I am calculating the nuances of gray in thunder. I am considering pebbles lost in a rot of fog. It is the hour of stained silver and lace communion dresses and wedding dresses frayed, stained. Why are such fabrics saved?

My canopied bed is waiting for me on the gallery floor. I cannot understand this juxtaposition. I think I am going insane. Can this be possible? Is my bed a feature of the exhibition?

"We must sell tickets," Diego whispers. I am being carried on a stretcher. I am dressed in Tehauna ruffles and have a blanket over my leg. Cristina applied the paints to my face and lips. They feel waxy, my skin refuses to absorb them. Diego stares at me with an intensity he ordinarily reserves for dessert menus. "Think of the publicity and the overhead."

I am transferred from the stretcher directly to my four-poster bed. I realize I am meant to be positioned in it and I am. The details of this event had not been revealed to me. But after the lampshades sewn from human skin, after the metal railing of the trolley car punched through my vagina, after the nurses ran from the operating room, spreading rumors that I was rank as a dead goat, that maggots were nesting in my abscesses, what is one more horror? Still, I want to get up, to explain that this is a completely unacceptable form of debasement.

"You have the sensitivity of sand," I tell Diego. He thanks me, kisses my hand. Then he is circulating through the gallery, patting and slapping backs, laughing, pressing the flesh, he calls it, and searching for commissions.

The gallery is overflowing. Inverted faces hang above me like a series of senseless bloated paper lamps. They are lamps in reverse. They suck out illumination and in return, give vacancy, a sudden stained void. They are staring down at the barely breathing ruin of Frida, displayed among her abnormal paintings. They will purchase them. Then Diego and I will buy corn and chickens. We will buy sequins and gardenias. We will feed our eunuchs and concubines. But I am unprepared for this, Frida, a lurid spectacle.

In my canopied bed on the floor of Galería del Arte Contemporáneo, I am surrounded by my canvases, my paintings on wood and metal. They are postcards from other points of entry and exit. They are from ports that do not yet exist. They have floated in a stasis. Other women who have successfully vanished will find them. They will recognize themselves in me. Trotsky was wrong. It is not the secret police you must fear. It is the ones you take for lovers, mouth to ochre mouth, calling one another dogs, begging to be wrapped in rags. Then you marry them. Divorce them. Later, they turn you in.

I thought Flora might come to the exhibit. Yes. I expected her. I calculated her age. She is twenty-two years old. She would wear leather boots, silver accents, and perhaps a silk scarf instead of a hat. She would have a metal hoop in her eyebrow or lip, a statement of fashion. Her hair would be free, unbrushed, behind her. She doesn't brush her hair because it takes too much time and she is always moving. Perhaps she could take a train here. She could get a ride from someone. She is the age I was when I first married Diego. Perhaps she has read about the exhibition in the newspaper. Perhaps it was mentioned at the university. Certainly, she is interested in a woman's art.

I am in my bed from my room in the Casa Azul. I am violated and afraid. I barely breathe. I do not shiver or cough. I am part of the installation. Is this the modern collective intimacy? I am a pear, a slice of melon on a plate. I am a still life. We wanted to be international. Now there is no privacy. That is why one must master disappearing. I smile with painted lips that feel embalmed. My face is artificial, a mask. Has Diego considered selling it?

I search the gallery for vanished women. Occasionally you can spot them at racetracks, where they frequently know which horses to bet. The gray ones with autumn names, with rain and bridges in them, harbors and drowned men. Names that evoke fluid demarcations.

Disappeared women often wear boots because they prefer walking. It is the only way to become intimate with a city. You must know it stone by stone like the body of a person you have loved. You must feel the boulevards curve beneath your feet like so many damaged spines. I have not yet disappeared. That is because I cannot walk. My toes have fallen off. I want Flora to come, bringing me boots that fit.

"Did we sell many tickets?" I whisper to Diego, and he nods yes. His face is inflated from the petits fours he has eaten and the promise of money.

We are circus refugees. We are in the ambulance because we are sick. We are driving back to the Casa Azul, the huge exhausted bear and his crippled diminutive. I am a parrot with nothing left to say. The enraged siren speaks for us. It's so modern.

Nothing can surprise anymore, but still, we are utterly spent. It reminds me of July afternoons when we drank tequila and made love. From the terrace, scalloped roofs with orange tiles. Green ocean. Churches or mosques on a hill. Diego discovering me like a child with a doll. The air was sea salt, sun, tequila, sweat, and fermenting sugarcane. Now, in the ambulance, I consider the atrocity in the gallery where I was more naked than a human being should be.

Diego and I were meant for a sideshow. I was the girl with the gold dust like islands forming in her gutters of wet flesh. He ate peanuts and sawdust, greasepaint, and sequins. That is how we found each other. But in the current arrangement, everything must play in the center. I wonder if my canopied bed will be left on the gallery floor. Where will I sleep? Diego is looking out the ambulance window, his eyes closed, hands resting on his belly. He is smiling in his sleep.

A stalled harbor. Paralyzed. Becalmed. The water is fragile, translucent, the texture of some intrinsic confusion that lingers. I am the river concluding in the sea. I am coming home.

Between a concussion of sky and ocean, elegant, like a suggestion of bleached violets, I have drifted to a seaport in mist. Perhaps all the inhabitants have vanished. And I cannot determine if what I hear is rain or waves. Does it matter? There is no actual line between drowning and communion.

It's a spring of remission. Morning is a sequence of tamed waves rising and falling like strings of clear glass bells. I paint in my wheelchair. In between the azure gulfs and eddies of morphine, I paint in my canopied bed. My bed was lost for a while, I don't remember how, but now it has been returned to me.

I paint fruit because it is strange and abnormal, the hideous melons, with their seeds like black tears, with their bodies moistening and losing definition. Poor watermelons, severed, amputated. Soon they will need wheelchairs.

Perhaps it is an elongated dusk. Waves break in lines like fingers, like the many arms of an obsolete deity. I consider the way prayers are intoned, how the human voice insinuates itself in air and forms imperceptible architectures. Perhaps these are the lost cities men habitually search for. They bloom in dusk by certain oceans where only disappeared women can see them.

"You will put yourself to sleep permanently doing this," Diego warns. But he does not stop me. He does not call Nurse. He lets me put Demerol into my vein myself. I do it better than Nurse. I am more accurate, more astute. My veins are like tributaries, and I know where the deep holes are, where to fish, where to stick in the metal.

"I must take it prophylactically, before the pain is too severe," I remind him. His face is grave.

"Chiquita, you may not wake up," Diego says. His voice is neutral.

"I am afraid," Cristina says. In her apron pocket, the rosary bulges like a strand of seedpods.

"Of course you are, " I say. "You're so conventional. What day is this?"

"It's a day beyond you," Cristina replies, remote, rubbing her pocket where Mother's rosary is curled.

What a moron. I've told her about Frank, playing guitar at the end of the universe. Is she without intelligence entirely?

"We must say good-bye," Cristina falters.

"Good-bye." It's not miraculous that I live. It's bad luck. It's tedious.

"I forgive you for everything, even what you did to Mother," Cristina says. "The anomalies of your condition. The morphine. It drove you insane."

"Thank you," I think I'm supposed to say. Diego glares at me. "You are generous," I add.

"Will you tell me again about the end? I will pay attention," Cristina says, each syllable an individual begging mouth. She widens her eyes.

"A stranger arrives in an isolated town in foothills of maple forest. Trees are turning henna and claret. Sunset is the russet of radium and fresh scars. And the pinks of flamingos. He stands on a veranda as a flock of burgundy jungle birds appears. He removes his clothes. A naked man, playing guitar in a rented room."

"That is all?" Cristina, so dim, so eager.

"Yes, sister." A pause in which summer grasses rise, tomatoes ripen. A clarification. Birds. Silence. Diego looks threatening.

"I forgive you also," I say. "Go now. Go and pray for me."

The compendium of clichés leaves. "Don't let her in again," I tell Diego.

Cristina will not be a vanished woman. She lacks daring and imagination. Vanished women know the various styles of archi-

tecture, both cities and gardens. They have mastered the intricacies of sudden navigation in places where they have not yet been.
They know how to not appear startled, how to take readings
from wind, how to compensate, and devise camouflage. They
carry gold coins etched with the faces of dead princes. They
know how to date objects from the past. They do this with car-
bon 14, which measures the half-life of radioactivity. Sometimes
they employ other methods, such as counting rings in trees and
the level of trapped pollens at the bottom of lakes. Cristina can
barely do arithmetic.

"What are you doing?" Diego asks. He is watching me with
my syringe, how steady my hand is, what archery.

"I am disappearing," I tell him.

He thinks I am alluding to death. He knows absolutely nothing of alternative parallel regions. He thinks there is only one
chronology. That is why he is living in a museum.

When a woman has disappeared, everything is intelligible,
human motivations and what wires carry. All impulses are equally
coherent and predictable. Once you have divested yourself of ordinary structure, once you have lost or abandoned symmetry and
body parts, once you have become more than subterranean, once
you have successfully reconstructed yourself one atom at a time,
you sense when storms are coming. You know when to warn fishermen. You determine this by a complex shift in the wind, an
unexpected confluence of cloud and fog. It is the residue of someone's terrible dream. That is what poisons the currents.

Vanished women have no fear of water. They are buoyant. They cannot drown or bloat. If lost at sea, they simply blink three times with concentration and a bridge rises fully formed from waves. They walk across it. That is why women who have disappeared often have watery professions. They are singers on ships. They live on barges, bringing oranges and cherries into cities. Sometimes they are laundrywomen or women married to fishermen.

Disappeared women are revered for their gambling skills. They know which numbers to play, that forty-seven, and I, Frida, am going to be forty-seven, is best for roulette and lotteries. They bet on horses and dogs. They love bullfights, cockfights, boxing matches between men. They sit in the first row. A woman with a hat and a partial veil. She demands ringside in a half-whisper, her accent impeccable, whatever the capital. No one could refuse her request.

"Do you have wishes?" Diego the priest asks. For a man constructing a monument to himself, performing last rites is a minor activity.

"Are you speaking of my birthday?" I counter, suspecting a trick. I know it is my birthday. I am forty-seven now. My sister has gone to buy me a present. "Or are you here in a larger sense?"

"I am here," Diego says. "I have been here twenty-five years."

It is true. We have been alone together for twenty-five years. So I tell him I wish for more Demerol. I almost reveal my regrets about Flora. But I don't. I stop myself.

"It's my birthday," I remind Diego.

"You've had your birthday, sweet one," Diego says.

They gave me a birthday party, yes. Cristina dressed and painted me and I was brought out, as if posthumously. I agreed to this because I thought it possible that Flora would come. I said to Diego and Cristina, repeatedly, "Invite everyone."

I was arranged on a sofa. I watched the door, waiting for a twenty-three-year-old woman in the chic uniform of an art student. They look the same, in London and Moscow and San Francisco. I wanted her to give me a birthday gift, leather boots, though I only need one, the left one. And her photograph. I would put it into a locket and wear it around my neck. They would bury me with it. And I wanted her kiss. Just one. And I would like to run my hands through her woven hair, each finger separating tendrils into tributaries, and she would run through me.

It is a night without increment, like a hospital night, but moist and expectant. It might negotiate. Inland, women stand in plazas, exposed in mist like powdered lilacs. Their mouths form shapes only vanished women can decipher. It is not a spasm of the lip, but an alphabet rendered in imperceptible sequences of breath. It is only offered at dusk. There are the obligatory cathedral bells turning the night pewter. In alleys, the siege of magenta bougainvillea against adobe buildings that seem too frail and transitory to contain them. I will tell Flora it is for this vertigo that we travel.

Flora Violetta is a woman now. She is modern. She lives in a just forming American city in California, perhaps. There the ocean is light blue and gauzy like something you could wrap a cut in. The air is a fine sea dust. Flora presents her face to the wind and it caresses and sculpts her.

"You are so far away, Chiquita," Diego says. "What are you thinking?"

"The awe," I manage.

"The grandeur? We loved it best," Diego remembers.

"And it loved us." I reach for his hand. He takes my fingers like they were tiny birds.

It is raining violently and suddenly. Clouds break open. Gutted bellies, seamless rain. This is serious water. Outside is an inverted bay, bold, vivid, like larkspur. Now there is lightning.

When I was Flora Violetta's age, when Diego was committing his necessary infidelities, I went alone to picture shows in San Francisco, Detroit, and New York. In the movie theaters everything became autumnal. Afternoons were thin slivers of tin like the coatings on bracelet amulets. It didn't matter what was being shown, romances, comedies, adventures, musicals. I did not care what Henry Ford or Leon Trotsky said about their value, their politics or intentions. It was the enclosure itself I loved, the patterned carpets, the profoundly maroon velvet curtains. It was a legal point of exit and entry. It was a port from which one might be lifted off the earth itself. I was ready to go. Just give me a word, a gesture, an indication, however small.

There was a possibility of rebirth in a light that was thin silver. I was a child hiding in a trunk in an attic under cotton summer curtains, and everyone was looking for me. But I had already sent my body into another hemisphere with a different time zone, so I could not speak to them. I could not be found.

Diego was on the scaffolds. He was fucking the mayor's mistress. He would have her assume the dog position. He offered her a collar and leash. She accepted with her mouth. Then he was teaching her what happens to women who offer themselves belly down. "The moon is your enemy," Diego told her. "The more of you I see, the more I can bruise."

I was pregnant with my daughter, Flora, though the doctors said it was not possible. My womb was gutted. In my belly, an alley of unfinished tenements and the tunnels fists make. The doctors said my pregnancy was a fantasy.

I would enter the motion picture houses in the late morning and stay through three showings, until the streets were pitch. The arrested November was a distillation, not of leaves precisely, but representations of leaves, a stylized sequence of perpetual slow falling. In the theater, there were no increments, no decisions, only the incalculable elegance of an autumn spent inside alone. Human love was peripheral.

There would be a dozen other men and women in the matinees. They were also alone. We formed a temporary electric community with our rituals of silence and privacy. We were like a church or hospital burn ward. We wore hats, scarves, bent into our coats. We did not look at each other's faces. That would have been a violation.

The images on the screen were small enough to be absorbed. Cinema contained only toy cars and toy ships and a paint that looked like blood but wasn't. No residue would remain when I left the theater six hours later. I would be untouched, a woman in the process of becoming permanently autumnal, like an out-of-focus photograph, formulated with chemicals in back rooms where there are only charcoals and gradations of silver. I wanted the cold to leak into my bones after my youth of palm trees and brilliant skinned skies that had contrived to murder me. I wanted some icy antidote.

I regretted when movies turned to color, which spoiled them. I preferred screens of black and white, grainy, in languages I did not speak. Movies with subtitles I did not read. I did not care what the characters were saying. I let the images flicker across my face like so many indifferent tongues. At such moments, I had the sensation I was falling in love. I felt Flora in my womb, a pewter fluttering, sailboats rising and dipping, and I patted her head of black hair.

"You are so far away," Diego repeats. He is holding my hand. He squeezes it with urgency. "Stay with me," he is saying.

My mouth fills with slow regret. There is too much autumn night, though I know it is just days after my birthday, it is July. "I am here," I somehow say. "I am still here." Why is it taking so long? I would like the wind to touch my face. I tell Diego to open the balcony windows, to pull back the curtains. I tell him I want autumn. That's the season for sick women.

Autumn is a remote lake beneath a coating of leaves like arched panels of glass in a noon cathedral. Day dissolves into chilled amber. Autumn with its danger and intrinsic absence arrives. It unfurls its silver banner, flag of the lame and solitary, and I recognize and salute it.

"It was a good birthday," Diego decides. He has not opened windows. It is July, humid. He has folders and books on his lap. He is wearing glasses.

It is my last birthday. I know this, of course. Everyone knows. That's why the ridiculous strained glee at the final fiesta. It was currents of hysteria. People do not know how to say good-bye to the dying, so everyone pretended I was fine. Just another relapse. I was dizzy, candlelight was a lurid brass. I put Demerol in my veins between the soup and fish courses. Twice I fell asleep. I scolded Diego, "Everyone is not here."

Then it is the next day and Diego wants to take me somewhere. To march with the Communists. To make a statement. It is raining. I put morphine in one wrist, then Demerol in a vein I find in my neck. Diego helps me slide vials and syringes into my coat pocket. I do not paint my face. I wear an ordinary cloth coat. Then Diego takes me in my wheelchair, the woman without a leg, to the demonstration. It will be the last time I feel wind.

"Must we do this?" I ask. I am in my wheelchair. The air is like glass.

"Yes, Frida. We are partners. It has biographical resonance." Diego pushes my wheelchair. "I'll take care of you."

It is raining, dull, insistent. We are protesting the CIA, its illicit presence in Guatemala. I have gone without my face painted, without a costume. An old woman at forty-seven, with a common coat and scarf tight around her head. I keep looking for Flora.

There are many students with banners of protest. She should be here. What if she doesn't recognize me? I should have insisted on my costume, my hibiscus and orchids, it's July, everything is blooming in the garden. I should have worn my tiers of tin and shell beads that cast miniature replicas of themselves on my face so I seem tattooed with symbols. Is it too late for my thick lipsticks that taste like dirty wax in my mouth?

Diego pushes my wheelchair. Perhaps, in the crowd, I will find other vanished women. And not just vanished women. On the periphery, on the border of fever and release, other things are possible.

For instance, everything is in season for missing children, for miscarried, aborted, and murdered children. They are not gone. They are riding cruise ships. It is the perpetual Caribbean. Islands are dots they connect with their relentless passage. They stand on deck, air tropical with plumeria, and wind in warm waves. When you are a vanished woman or child, you can buy gardenias and peonies even on winter Sundays in rain, even when the roads to the capital are closed by flood and the harbor deserted.

"Each time you overdose, each hospital, they report this," Diego says, stern. "They trade in rumor. They suspect suicide. They sell their opinions to newspapers."

"Is it bad for sales?" I ask.

I have woken after my birthday and the CIA protest in the rain. I have pneumonia. Diego threatens to take my cigarettes. He forces them from my hand. I threaten to jump out the window. He gives them back. He paces up and down my bedroom, picking up and putting down jewelry boxes and dolls and carvings, framed photographs, a tarot deck, a ball of yarn. What is he searching for?

He cannot find it. I have taken all the compass points, all the tools for navigation, all the manmade instruments. When you reemerge, when you have been reassembled, as if by blind men from scraps, you finally know where you're going.

Vanished women often get tattoos of a singular crescent moon on their neck. Or a cluster of hearts like a rash on their thigh. They procure a passport in the name of a jewel or a fragrant flower. Camellia. Jade. Hyacinth. Rose. They list their occupation as student. They say they are self-employed. They smile. Their mouths are lined with Dragon Lady red lipstick. They are processed without delay.

"It is very bad," Diego announces. "The incessant innuendo. The suicide rumors in this heathen region. The church has an ear everywhere. The ugly gossip. I am most concerned."

Each time I return from too much morphine, too much Demerol, I have more knowledge. I understand vanished women have skin that changes with the seasons, particularly if the woman disappeared with a brutal severing. This is why one must strive for small methodical points of exit. Something the size a needle might make. You must avoid the obvious. You must not create a scene. You must make a clean departure. You don't want them burning candles in the windows and reciting your name out loud. Such gestures and their glare give the disappeared migraines.

"Are we talking about points of exit?" I think I am asking, but there is so much harbor, such enormity and weight, and I am under it. My eyes are languid and stained and milky, like a sea creature. I can read etchings in rocks now, and the traces left by weeds in sand. Is it possible forests grow at the bottom of warm oceans? Lime orchards in rows? A ring of sixty apple trees turning rouge? Is this what we feel just beneath us as we swim? What rustles like moths, grazes our flesh, and why we are afraid?

"Frida. You must listen now," Diego is saying, holding a book of animal glyphs. "Fucking whore. Sit up."

I will vanish with the simple elegance of smoke. When I return, no one will recognize me. I will not have to camouflage myself with costumes that are not warm enough in autumn. I will have no deformities, no wounds that don't heal. I will be a woman who wears tailored suits and five-inch high heels like stilettos. And skirts that stop above the knee, silk panties with transparent panels, and tennis dresses. I want fishnet stockings. I am a water woman. I must have these nets. I demand this.

"I have fixed it with the doctor," Diego says. "You are very sick. You coughed up one entire lung. Your fever is monumental. The doctor will call it an embolism." Diego produces a note from the stacks of paper, which are not glyphs. Words. He reads it out loud. "Pulmonary embolism. He has promised this to me."

KATE BRAVERMAN

"There will be no repercussions?" I must be absolutely clear.

"It will be clean enough for the pope," Diego says with enthusiasm.

When I disappear, I will dress like women in New York, with tweeds and gabardines, and trim square velvet hats. I will have limbs that match. I will wear shorts and swimming suits such as women now do in the south of France. I will have a bicycle with a basket attached to the bars. I will put my breads and cheese and pears in it.

I will purchase a bicycle for Flora. We will be fifteen together, best friends, with layers of tea rose on our necks, and lips a frost pink like taffy. We will ride our bicycles to the river, find shade beneath an oasis of oak. We will eat chocolates and, touching with our shoulders, study wedding gowns in magazines.

Women who have vanished find their eyes have altered. In winter, they wear the shades of bruises, violets, lavenders, grays. My eyes will be sapphire. I will be a flame in your living room. I will be the only light on your patio. You won't need more.

I will spend three months in summer in Acapulco. It will be Flora's vacation from the university. We will rent a villa with borders of hibiscus. My skin will turn burnt orange and burnt auburn. My hair will turn red. Everyone will say, Frida, you are so exquisite, you look carved. And there is nothing eccentric in your appearance. You have become quite normal. And your daughter, Flora, well she is an amulet.

Now it is a night of jasmine and lavender. I am ash blond. Diego is falling in love with me all over again. It's as if he's been blasted by a bullet. He falls on the floor, on the ground, into the dirt. We embrace and burrow in. Diego is kneeling in prayer. Or perhaps bending over a table near me. A large glass bottle. We are getting drunk together. It is a gesture with a further implication. Perhaps he means to say he will love me in future autumns. Perhaps he has found Flora. That is why we are celebrating.

Autumn lacks a border. You don't know it's winter until your hair turns raven. My skin will be translucent and I will suggest that Diego call me Pearl. The individual arteries in my arms will be like threads in a fabric. I must be partially vanished already because they are visible now. They are pulsing. If anyone saw my arms they would think of rivers and boulevards and borders crossed by deception. They would think of smuggled contraband and morphine. I show my arms to Diego. They flutter from my body like rags.

"Do you know the name for this?" I ask.

I am webbed with morphine kisses. Demerol kisses. This is the mouth I have sought and at last found. I am minutely engraved with fine lines like the ink of a last will and testament. Butterflies cluster along my veins. They drink from me like coyotes at dusk water holes. I have gardens on my arms. I have canals. Legion are the creatures I feed.

Diego turns away. He places his hands over his eyes to cover them. He is hiding his eyes. He says, "No." But I cannot remember what we are discussing. A corridor of geometric tiles and mirrors? A patio of lapis lazuli? Are we planning another house?

Diego is doing something with a bottle. We are getting drunk together. He has brought the best goblets, the ones Trotsky's wife gave me in exchange for her husband. He has taken the New Year's Eve champagne from his cellar. I am flapping my arms. I say, "This is how you drown standing up."

He cannot hear me. So much of me has already vanished. I belong now to the seasons. I will wear felt hats with feathers and veils. It will always be autumn, gray with constant storms and cigarette smoke.

After I disappear, I will be utterly different. You could not pick me out of a lineup. I will be the sort of woman who quietly reads Spanish poetry in rooms where shadows collect. Anyone who encounters me would think only of bridges across ancient rivers. And folklore known only by intuition and rumor. They would realize they have opened the wrong door.

"Are you ready?" Diego asks, holding a prism in fat bear paws that are shaking.

"Yes. No." Syllables and their opposites. I am waves, I rise and rock. Words are charms or sails or stones. You offer verbal amulets to the air, to your husbands, and to circumstance.

"One for the road," Diego says. He pours the New Year's Eve champagne into my glass, into his glass. It's another party.

When I have vanished, the elements will conceal and define me. The weather will determine my moods, my physical appearance, the way my hair can turn from flame to ash blond during the course of one sudden brutal thought. Perhaps I will not breathe in a conventional sense, but will be somehow plugged in, like a lamp, or turned on with a key like a car.

Diego and I are having a private New Year's Eve party. Curious, we haven't invited anybody. Nurse has gone away. I can tell. There is more air in my bedroom. If someone spoke my name now, with urgency, surprising me, my hair might fall out.

There must be no intrusion. I must remember. I have no fear of bridges, transition, solitude, or the subconscious. I know the names of all the rivers in all the capitals, and the seas and oceans they eventually meet. I have seen women on terraces above alleys, and their eyes are the only light for a thousand miles. I have seen women like plants, fed directly from the sun. They are like rare Brazilian orchids who root in air, hang in wind like seaweed in waves. I can see this through the mesh of my veil or my mantilla. I can see this by looking through glass. It is a glass I am holding now and Diego is encouraging me to drink.

"I drink to drown my sorrows," I used to say at parties on Fifth Avenue. "But the damn things have learned to swim."

The Demerol waters are too deep for any living thing. After the vanishing, after I have found the perfect and untraceable sublife, I will know what the harbors are trying to say. I will know which coast to walk beside, which waves to let caress me to the thigh, which lullabies, which muted chrome litanies. I will decipher the currents effortlessly. I know what each brings. Mangoes. A string of amber pearls. Two punctured truck tires. A colossus of halved clamshells. Parts of an umbrella and cello. I will have two legs. All my accumulations will glitter.

"I will hold you," Diego says. Ah, Diego, the gallant. I open my arms. I pull him into me. Now I see. Not a prism in his hands but a glass syringe. He fills it with bottles of Demerol.

Crinoline, taffeta, chiffon. This is what vanished daughters wear. Flora wears leather with fringe and metal studs. She is studying law in London. Or she is a singer in Los Angeles. She has a band with a name containing mythological resonances and properties, like Witch Hazel. Flora thinks herself more exotic than her friends, more eclectic and smart. She considers herself more modern. Her thoughts are electric, rapid, interconnected. They burn like radium lamps. She is not afraid of the dark.

"I hope for a happy exit and I hope never to come back," I tell Diego. Or not back in a form you recognize.

"That's a suave exit line. They'll remember that." Diego smiles. He holds my hand. He kisses it.

"Thank you. Good luck on your museum," I say.

Diego considers this. "Do you think it's too bold? Too flagrant?" he asks.

"No, my darling. Not at all. It suits you," I lie. Poor Diego. A man with the sensibility of pond scum.

He sticks the syringe with the many bottles of Demerol into a patch of skin he finds on my thigh. I watch. It does not hurt. Our bodies are ultramarine like suffering and sweet masks and returning to the terrace in the last light, in a stalled transparency, longing for boats and splendor. Free fall and we know the violets and the postures of loss in winter. Diego. How we talked of love and awe while leaves scattered in complications of violet and jade. When we beat the linens clean on rock and draped teeth around our necks like captured moons. Before free fall and blistered autumn, when our lips became maps of where the taint lies. That was before the hard ceremonies, when we were cold and gave testament, when we swam out to meet all the ships, when we stood on terraces annointed by rain, when we lived in a country of rivers that had all names.

Now I see. It is a young woman. She has a husband. She wears his wedding ring. They live in a stone house on a hill overlooking a maple forest and further, a harbor. It's a hundred-and-fifty-year-old farmhouse in a northern region with an extreme climate and too much rain. The house is surrounded by an old orchard of sixty apple trees. In this way, she is married on the inside and out. She has two rings.

The wooden porch is extravagant with lilac and wisteria. There is a colossus of darkness beyond the porch. There are occasional lights on the winding road and beyond, lighthouses. But when it is cloudy, they can't see this.

In the front room, what might be heirloom furniture. She collects milagros, tin hands, feet, guns, crows, hearts, corncobs, and knives. She is saving them for a project she has not quite devised. She collects seashells in glass jars labeled Maui and St. Lucia. Seashells like children's fingernails, like white moons that are startled.

Their walls are a forest of paintings. Canvases are hung from floor to ceiling. They lean in stacks against closets, as if waiting their turn. Stone and wooden sculptures are on tables and shelves and stuck in kitchen cabinets with the sugar and flour. In the pantry beside sacks of beans are ceramic bowls, statues, bells, dolls, and stacks of photographs and maps they don't look at.

Night is silver and specific. The rain makes it so. A clarification occurs. The apples are a mesh, the moonlight a catalyst. The air in their rooms is glassy, fragrant, and rare. It could be distilled. You could keep it in a crystal decanter.

Below, a stream, many acres, at least two hundred, and a greenhouse for growing orchids and poppies. They have a pair of white dogs, albino shepherds. They have no television. At night, in their bed upstairs, windows open, flower and vegetable gardens blow in the scent of rose hips and tomato leaves and summer ocean, vaguely citrus. She reads him poetry in Spanish, Neruda and Paz. He reads American adventure novels to her while night darkens. When he reads to her, she places her head on his shoulder and grips his hair, the skin on his thighs tight with her fingers.

"Didn't they read you bedtime stories?" her husband teases. He already knows the answer. There are novels he has read to her thirty and forty times. Her delight. How she says, "Again. Oh, please."

It is July. Her hands are tanned from gardening. The tulips, peonies, and lilacs have passed. Now the apples are brilliant as lanterns, glazed and inflamed. The limbs of the apple trees remind her of silks and brocades, the patterns of kimonos on engravings. The foxglove is a deep purple, and hollyhocks have risen a pink that looks like painted adobe. Soon they'll have corn and tomatoes and carrots. She is turning into her husband, curving into him, holding him as he sleeps. He is the berth. He anchors her. She swims to him, embraces him with the length of her body, and the drift subsides.

The woman is restless, slides out of bed, walks softly downstairs. She has insomnia and nightmares. Recently she dreamt she was lost in the grasses near the vegetable garden. The apple trees were studded with what she thought were illuminated cocoons. She counted them. There were sixty-seven. She approached queasy and trembling. Then she realized the cocoons were actually infants, stillborns. They were strung up to the limbs with razor wire. They were hanging on metal hooks, moonlight on their bellies making them gold as coins. Their languid dead eyes were facing the same direction. Some infants were moaning and mewing like fox.

"This is C-section farmland," a woman she could not recognize was saying.

She smokes. She drinks vodka and brandy, takes amphetamines and sleeping pills. Often, she paces the house, examines the edges and shadows, reaches her hand behind the curtains, opens doors, studies the porch, the front lawn. She expects something.

She likes to walk barefoot at night, when her husband is sleeping and there are fireflies and stars. She might live a whole other life while her husband is asleep. She craves the warm rain. The vegetable garden is behind a five-foot-high slatted wood fence her husband built, to keep out deer. She painted the wood white. It gleams in darkness. She opens the gate that is arched, thick with clematis and climbing roses. Only the peas and straw-berries are ripe. She picks handfuls, bends over and rapidly crowds them into her mouth. Sometimes she eats so much, so fast, she vomits.

The rain is lighter, barely perceptible. She removes her nightgown, lets the breeze take it. She crawls on the ground between corn and tomato plants. She lies face up to the clouded sky, waiting.

Today sunset was an extravaganza. The sky was like the backs of agitated flamingoes. Suddenly, a flock of burgundy jungle birds flew in the direction of the new tenant on West Harbor Road. He plays guitar at dusk. Sometimes she hears fragments of melody between crows and owls. A suggestion of foghorn. Dog. Car. Coyote. Thunder over the ocean. The abrupt thrashing and sighing of deer. All of this forms a mesh, she thinks, our private aviaries. She is naked, her back muddy, her mouth open wide, a pile of peas and strawberries on her belly.

In town, they think she is eccentric, vulgar, and intriguing. They say she is secretive and reckless. She drives a red Cadillac with a license plate that reads IN AWE. She blasts rock and roll from the car stereo, as if wanting to teach something to the air. She hits her brakes with a force that makes dust clouds form. She collects speeding tickets. Her license has been suspended. She has been seen in her vegetable garden wearing a bikini and stiletto high heels. Her lawn appears covered with mole holes. Her skin turns burnt orange and almond, then bronze. She does not burn in the sun.

People discuss her abrasive voice, how corrosive it is, loud and coarse, like she'd been eating gravel. Its harshness suprises, seems superimposed, not her at all. Perhaps it's a genetic defect. Perhaps she has stitches in her throat. But why does she not brush her hair? Why does she dye it red, blond, charcoal? And the way she applies cosmetics. It's as if she smeared fire-engine-red lipstick on her mouth without using a mirror. It's unfortunate because she has beautiful white teeth. She is still, in her oddness, attractive.

She rides a bicycle with her husband. They wind down to the harbor where they have a sailboat. On summer Sundays, she packs a lunch for them, carries it in her bicycle basket. They sail past midnight. Their boat has no name, no homeport. Sometimes they swim. They set up croquet on their acres of front lawn facing the harbor. They play tennis at the country club where they do not speak to anyone. They have been observed reading on a porch swing. For them, it is always Sunday.

It is said that she has extreme moods. Sometimes she dominates conversations with opinion and anecdote. Don't get her started on politics or art. She'll give you a lecture in the parking lot of the general store and talk your ear off. Be careful, too. She has unexpected areas of expertise. You'd be surprised.

Then there are interludes when she doesn't speak at all. She remains indoors, staring out windows, wrapped in a woolen shawl, weeping. There are fifteen windows facing the ocean and she has been seen crying in all of them. Her face is a tragic embodiment of autumn, a darker charcoal outline behind cigarette smoke and clouds dull as asphalt.

No one knows where they are from or how long they are staying. They simply appeared six years ago. No one visits them. They do not volunteer for community projects. They do not go to church. They have declined hiking, gardening, and the theater club. She refused to even take a pamphlet describing town organizations. They do not support the library or the beautification of Main Street. They do not subscribe to the Sunday newspaper. They do not receive mail. They say they're retired. No one believes them.

Rumors persist. She's a gypsy from Los Angeles. Her family is dead. She's a drug addict. She has a terminal illness. She was a nun. She's an alcoholic. She's Jewish. She trades stocks on the computer. She bets on horseraces. She has amnesia from a car crash. She can decipher tarot cards. She's been on stage. She's been in prison. She speaks unusual languages. She has a substantial inheritance. She collects gold coins. She has an astrologer. She takes tango lessons. She can read palms and dreams.

The woman is amused by the gossip. She is naked in warm mud, eating rain-wet strawberries and peas. The ground feels like clay and she digs her toes into it, how the damp briefly holds and then releases, holds, releases. Darkness is a matter of strata. She is a geologist of night. The new tenant, Frank, is playing guitar, fragments of rhythm infiltrate the air.

She carries a bottle of brandy and a pack of cigarettes. She laughs because she is aroused by the strangeness of the sound, how it rushes from the soles of her feet and breaks out of her mouth in spasms. She offers her laughter to the enormous confederation of cloud and shadow, smoke and melody that is night. When there is lightning, she chases it. When there is thunder she howls.

She does not remember Frida.

ABOUT THE AUTHOR

Kate Braverman is a native of Los Angeles who grew up surrounded by the counterculture of San Francisco. She has published three novels—*Wonders of the West* (1993), *Palm Latitudes* (1988), and *Lithium for Medea* (1979)—four books of poetry—*Postcards from August* (1990), *Hurricane Warnings* (1987), *Lullaby for Sinners* (1980), and *Milkrun* (1977)—and a collection of stories, *Squandering the Blue* (1990). She won the O. Henry Award in 1992 for her short story, "Tall Tales from the Mekong Delta." Braverman lives in upstate New York with her husband, the biologist Alan Goldstein, and her daughter, Gaby.